W9-AZY-311

"So How Do You Intend To Play This In Front Of My Family And Yours?"

Mohab took Jala's hands to his lips. "I intend to show everyone how proud I am to be your intended, that this was a hope I had since I first saw you."

She withdrew her hands. "No need to go overboard or you'll only make them suspicious."

She didn't believe him. He hadn't thought of marriage in the years he'd craved her from afar, since he'd never thought marriage was in the cards for him at all.

But now, with the turn his life had taken, everything was different. He'd come here still not clear about what he wanted beyond that he wanted her for as long as he could have her. Now he wanted everything. "So your original agreement stands as is?"

He held his breath. Hoping against hope...

Then she breathed, "Yes."

* * *

Seducing His Princess is part of the
Married By Royal Decree series:
When the king commands, they say "I do!"

* * *

If you're on Twitter,
tell us what you think of Harlequin Desire!
#harlequindesire

Dear Reader,

When I wrote my very first Harlequin Desire novel, *The Desert Lord's Baby,* I created Judar, the desert kingdom that was the cornerstone of my sheikhdom universe. And in those first magical three books about those irresistible brothers, one figure stood in the wings, talked about but never present. It was the Aal Masood princes' youngest sibling, their only sister, Jala.

For years, she'd refused to tell me her story. But she was so adamant in escaping my curiosity that I started to suspect her secrets were deep, dark and painful. And that made sure I'd never forget about her, and that I'd keep after her until I could discover her past trauma, and be there for her future happily every after.

But for years, I didn't know how to do that!

Enter Mohab Aal Ghaanem. Like a desert storm, he swept back into her life against all odds, even against her will. Their turbulent past stood like an insurmountable barrier, blocking the way to even mere forgiveness. Not that that could have stopped him. Mohab was an unstoppable force to Jala's immovable object. And I delighted in documenting their passionately explosive and emotionally tempestuous journey back to each other and to happiness. I hope you enjoy it as much!

I love to hear from readers, so email me at oliviagates@gmail.com, and please follow me on Facebook at my fan page, www.facebook.com/oliviagatesauthor, on Goodreads under Olivia Gates and on Twitter: @OliviaGates.

Thanks for reading!

Olivia

SEDUCING
HIS PRINCESS

—

OLIVIA GATES

HARLEQUIN® DESIRE

If you purchased this book without a cover you should be aware that this book is stolen property. It was reported as "unsold and destroyed" to the publisher, and neither the author nor the publisher has received any payment for this "stripped book."

Recycling programs
for this product may
not exist in your area.

ISBN-13: 978-0-373-73303-3

SEDUCING HIS PRINCESS

Copyright © 2014 by Olivia Gates

All rights reserved. Except for use in any review, the reproduction or utilization of this work in whole or in part in any form by any electronic, mechanical or other means, now known or hereafter invented, including xerography, photocopying and recording, or in any information storage or retrieval system, is forbidden without the written permission of the publisher, Harlequin Enterprises Limited, 225 Duncan Mill Road, Don Mills, Ontario M3B 3K9, Canada.

This is a work of fiction. Names, characters, places and incidents are either the product of the author's imagination or are used fictitiously, and any resemblance to actual persons, living or dead, business establishments, events or locales is entirely coincidental.

This edition published by arrangement with Harlequin Books S.A.

For questions and comments about the quality of this book, please contact us at CustomerService@Harlequin.com.

® and TM are trademarks of Harlequin Enterprises Limited or its corporate affiliates. Trademarks indicated with ® are registered in the United States Patent and Trademark Office, the Canadian Trade Marks Office and in other countries.

Printed in U.S.A.

Books by Olivia Gates

Harlequin Desire

  The Sarantos Secret Baby #2080
***To Touch a Sheikh* #2103
  A Secret Birthright #2136
Ω*The Sheikh's Redemption* #2165
Ω*The Sheikh's Claim* #2183
Ω*The Sheikh's Destiny* #2201
§*Temporarily His Princess* #2231
§*Conveniently His Princess* #2255
  Claiming His Own #2265
§*Seducing His Princess* #2290

Silhouette Desire

**The Desert Lord's Baby* #1872
**The Desert Lord's Bride* #1884
*The Desert King #1896
Δ*The Once and Future Prince* #1942
Δ*The Prodigal Prince's Seduction* #1948
Δ*The Illegitimate King* #1954
  Billionaire, M.D. #2005
  In Too Deep #2025
    "The Sheikh's Bargained Bride"
**To Tame a Sheikh #2050
***To Tempt a Sheikh* #2069

*Throne of Judar
ΔThe Castaldini Crown
**Pride of Zohayd
ΩDesert Knights
§Married by Royal Decree

Other titles by this author
available in ebook format.

OLIVIA GATES

has always pursued creative passions such as singing and handicrafts. She still does, but only one of her passions grew gratifying enough, consuming enough, to become an ongoing career—writing.

She is most fulfilled when she is creating worlds and conflicts for her characters, then exploring and untangling them bit by bit, sharing her protagonists' every heart-wrenching heartache and hope, their every heart-pounding doubt and trial, until she leads them to an indisputably earned and gloriously satisfying happy ending.

When she's not writing, she is a doctor, a wife to her own alpha male and a mother to one brilliant girl and one demanding Angora cat. Visit Olivia at www.oliviagates.com.

To my endlessly loving and supportive mother.
Thank you for being there for me always.
Love you, always.

Prologue

Six years ago...

A fist of foreboding squeezed Mohab Aal Ghaanem's
heart.

Najeeb was back. And Jala had gone to see him.

Although he had contrived to keep her from seeing Najeeb for months now as part of his original mission to keep
them apart, when Najeeb had returned in spite of all his
machinations, there'd been nothing further Mohab could
do. Nothing but demand Jala not see Najeeb.

And what reason could he have given for asking her not
to see his cousin and crown prince? That he was jealous?

She would have been shocked by the notion. At best,
this would have made her think he didn't trust her, or that
he wasn't the progressive man she thought him to be. Personal freedom and boundaries were very touchy subjects
with her, and she had serious issues with the "repressive
male dinosaurs" prevalent in their culture.

At worst, she might have suspected that he had other motives for wanting to prevent that meeting with her "best friend," motives that went beyond simple possessiveness. As he did.

So he'd stood back and watched her leave for that dreaded yet inevitable rendezvous. And she hadn't returned.

Not that she'd said she would. Having an early business meeting the next day close to her house in Long Beach, it made sense for her to spend the night at her home. He wished he could have waited for her there, but though she'd given him keys, the gesture had been only as a token of trust. She'd been adamant about not making their relationship public knowledge before she was ready to do so. He was probably working himself up for nothing but…

B'Ellahi… What was he *thinking?* It *was* for nothing. Jala had agreed to marry him. She was his, body and heart. He'd been her first, and he'd always be her only. He should have stopped worrying about how their relationship had started long ago, shouldn't have tried to keep Najeeb away once his…purpose had been achieved—even if the way it had been had taken him by surprise. He'd already been attracted to Jala, but he surely hadn't imagined when he'd first approached her that he'd fall for her that hard, that totally.

Emptying his lungs, he strode away from the window. He could barely make out anything from sixty floors up anyway.

Though he was sure he would have seen her.

Since he'd first laid eyes on her, she'd been the only one he ever truly saw, even when others should have been in his focus. As on the day of the hostage crisis, when he'd been sent to save Najeeb and had saved Jala, too.

Najeeb. Again. Everything always came back to him.

Mohab had kept his cousin away from New York, away

from Jala, for as long as possible. Any more contrivances would have made Najeeb suspect he was being manipulated. And since there were only a handful of people who had enough power to keep the crown prince of Saraya jumping—his father, King Hassan, his brothers and Mohab himself—Najeeb would have eventually drawn the proper conclusions.

By elimination, only Mohab, as the kingdom's top secret-service agent, had the skills and resources to invade Najeeb's privacy, to rearrange his plans, to nudge him wherever he wanted. The next step would have been finding out *why*.

So Mohab had been forced to let his cousin come back. To let Jala go to him. At nine o'clock this morning. That had been eleven hours ago.

What could be taking her so long?

Kaffa. Enough. Why not just call her instead of having a full-blown obsessive episode?

So he did. And it went straight to voice mail. Time and again.

When another hour passed and she hadn't called back, he tore out of his penthouse, numb with dread.

By the time he arrived at her house his nerves had snapped, one at a time. What if she was lying unconscious or unable to reach her phone? What if she'd been mugged… or worse? She was so beautiful, and he'd seen how men looked at her. What if someone had followed her home?

He barged inside and was hit at once with the certainty. She was there. Her presence permeated the place.

He ran upstairs, homing in on her. As he approached her bedroom, he heard sounds. To his distraught ears, they sounded like distress. Coming from the bathroom.

He tore inside. And there she was. In the shower cubicle. Facing the door. She saw him as soon as he saw her.

At his explosive entry, she lurched, her steam-obscured

face contorting, her lips parting. He assumed she'd gasped or even cried out. He could hear nothing now above the cacophony of his own turmoil and the spray of water. All he knew was that she was here. She was safe.

And he was tearing off his clothes, his only need to prove to himself both facts.

Then he was inside the cubicle, dragging her into his arms, groaning as he felt her warm resilience slamming against his aching flesh, her cry shuddering through him as he drove trembling hands into her soaked tresses, his feverish gaze roaming her water-streaked face. That face, that body, that essence, had taken control of his fantasies from the instant he'd seen her, from the very moment he'd claimed her. And she'd claimed him right back. Throughout these past five months, with each caress, with each passion-filled encounter, he found himself craving her more and more. His hunger for her knew no bounds.

"Mohab..."

He swallowed her gasp, drove his tongue inside her fragrant, delicious depths and she started squirming, building his fire higher. He needed to be inside her, possessing her, pleasuring her. Reassuring himself she was whole and all his.

His hand glided between her smooth thighs, sought her core. His fingers slid between her slick folds, and his head almost burst with the sledgehammer of arousal. Knowing she would love his urgency, that the edge of discomfort his ferocity would cause would amplify her pleasure, he cupped her perfect buttocks and opened her silky thighs around his hips. Capturing her lips again and again in ravaging kisses, he sought her entrance, flexed then sheathed himself in her molten tightness in one long, forceful thrust.

The sharpness of her cry, a testament to the intensity of her enjoyment, heightened his frenzy, her hot gust of passion expanding in his own lungs. Then he withdrew and pistoned back, needing to merge with her, dissolve in her, knowing it would send her berserk. It was unraveling him, too—acute sensations layering with every plunge, ratcheting with each withdrawal. The carnal groans torn from their depths rode him higher and higher. He felt his climax hurtling from his very essence, felt her shuddering uncontrollably, heard the sound of her tortured squeals telling him she'd explode in ecstasy if he gave her the cadence and force she needed.

Unable to prolong this torment a second more, he gave it to her, his full force behind his jackhammering thrusts, until she convulsed in his arms and her shrieks of pleasure snapped his own tension. He all but felt himself detonate in a violent release, the most intense he'd ever felt, his seed burning through his length, jetting into her depths to mingle with her own gushing climax.

At last, the severity of sensations leveled, leaving him so satiated, so depleted, he could barely stand. She collapsed in his arms as she always did. Taking her down to the floor, he soothed her, and she surrendered to his ministrations, letting him fondle and suckle her, pour wonder and worship all over her.

Then he carried her out of the shower and dried them both off. As he bent to take her to bed, she pushed out of his arms, unsteadily waddling away to fetch her bathrobe.

He winced. How insensitive could he be? He'd scared her witless bursting in here, made her limp with satiation for hours and could only think of continuing their intimacies?

He put on his pants as she turned to him, wrapped in the stark white bathrobe, her golden flesh glowing in contrast. The need to ravish her again almost overpowered him.

"What was *that* all about?"

He saw the hardness in her eyes before he heard it in her tone. Something he'd never been exposed to before.

Suddenly wary, he shrugged. "Wasn't it self-evident?"

"Not to me. What brought you here in the first place?"

Disturbed by her coldness, especially after the inferno they'd just shared, he told her what he could. At the tail end of his account, he released a breath he hadn't realized he'd been holding. "And then I found you in there and all I could think was that you're safe. And I was, as always, starving for you." He tried a coaxing smile. "Finding you already unwrapped was most opportune."

"So you thought it was okay to barge in here and just have your way with me?"

The harsh accusation hit him between the eyes. She'd never been angry with him before. And to be so for the first time today, of all days, jarred him.

He found his own voice hardening. "You loved every second. You came so hard you blew my brains out."

She shrugged, not contesting that truth, those molten-gold eyes growing harder. "The point is, you disregarded my choice. Your overriding tactics have become a pattern."

"What 'overriding tactics'?"

"All your manipulation, ending with trying to keep me from seeing Najeeb. You think I'm so oblivious I didn't notice? Oh, I noticed, all right…every time you nudged and cajoled. Every time you artfully overruled me. You're almost undetectable, but I've had enough time and proximity to decipher your methods."

So she'd caught on.

Either he'd underestimated her astuteness…or he couldn't keep a cool enough head around her to maintain the seamless subterfuge he normally employed in his professional life.

Coming clean wasn't an option, though. He couldn't let her know why he'd originally approached her, or how he'd kept Najeeb away, or why. He couldn't risk that she might suspect the genuineness of his current involvement. They already had too much working against their relationship to introduce internal strife. The feud that had long raged between their families was enough of an obstacle on its own. He had to deny any culpability. There was just too much at stake.

"Why would I want to stop you from seeing Najeeb?"

She glared up at him, then turned and walked out.

Unable to believe she'd turned her back on him, he watched her, that fist of foreboding squeezing his insides again.

Mohab finished dressing, then followed her into her bedroom. His mind churning, he approached her where she stood across the room in jeans and a T-shirt, raven hair starting to dry into a waterfall of gloss, looking heart-breakingly perfect.

"I'm sorry I got carried away in there," he started. "I didn't think you'd mind…didn't think at all. I've never been so frightened in my life, and I overreacted…."

"I could have said stop. I didn't. So let's drop it."

"Let's not. If you're angry with me, don't just freeze me out." He stopped before her, ran a finger down her velvet cheek. "I beg your forgiveness, *ya habibati,* if you felt I was disregarding your choices. I didn't mean to, and I—"

"Don't." Her interruption was exasperated this time. "It doesn't matter. I actually think it's a good opportunity to finally tell you what I've been putting off for too long."

"Tell me what?"

"That I wasn't in any condition to make a rational decision when I accepted your marriage proposal."

His heart faltered. "What do you mean?"

"I was experiencing a postsex high for the first time, which was heightened by the fact that I was already in-debted to you for saving my life during the hostage crisis. So when you hit me with your proposal, I found myself saying yes. I've tried to take it back ever since, but you wouldn't let me."

"You did no such thing." Denial rasped out of him. He shook his head, as if to snap out of the nightmare. "Is this why you kept putting off telling anyone about us? Not because you were afraid our families' feud would impact our relationship, but because you were having second thoughts?"

"I'm not just having second thoughts. I'm *certain* I don't want to get married."

That was it? A case of commitment phobia? That was something he could deal with.

He drew a breath of relief into his tight chest. "I can understand your wariness. You struggled for your independence. You might think you'd lose it with marriage. But I'll never encroach on your freedoms...." At her baleful glance, he insisted, "Whatever my transgressions, they were unintended. Guide me in navigating your comfort zones and I'll always abide by them. If I pushed you into a commitment too soon, I'll wait until you're ready."

"I'll never be ready to marry *you*."

He stared at her, beyond shocked, the ferocity of her rejection an ax cleaving into his heart.

Just yesterday, he'd thought everything was perfect between them. And she'd had all this resentment seething inside her? How had he been so oblivious?

This led him to the only possible explanation. A dreadful one. "Have you received a better offer?"

At his rough whisper, she turned away again. He wanted to pounce on her, to roar that she couldn't do this to him, to them. He remained paralyzed, sick electricity arcing in his clenched fists, jumbling his heart's rhythm.

He forced more mutilating deductions from numb lips. "Since this is coming right after you visited Najeeb, I assume he finally popped the question."

She bent to pick up her laptop, as if she'd already dismissed him from her life. Heartache morphed into fury, all his early, long-forgotten suspicions about the nature of her relationship with Najeeb crashed into his mind.

"That's why you wheedled into his life, isn't it? But then he left, and you thought he wouldn't come through, and you were…what? Keeping me as plan B in case he didn't propose? And now you got the offer you were after all along, the one where you become a future queen, and I'm suddenly redundant?"

She turned the eyes of a total stranger to him. "I'd hoped we could part on civil terms."

"Civil?" His growl sounded like a wounded beast's. "You expect me to stand aside and let you marry my cousin?"

"I expect you to know you have no say in what I do."

And he went mad with pain and rage. "You can't just toss me aside and hook up with him. In fact, you can forget it. Najeeb will withdraw his offer as soon as I tell him how I made you…ineligible to be his princess. Regularly, hard and long, for five months. That I even took you after you said yes to him."

Her eyes filled with something he'd never dreamed he'd see in them. Loathing. "And I expected you to take my decision like a gentleman. But I'm glad you showed me how vicious and dishonorable you can be when you're thwarted. Now I know beyond a shadow of a doubt that I was right to end this."

His blood congealed as she turned away. "You really think you *can* end it…just like that?"

Hearing his butchered growl, she turned at the door. "Yes. And I hope you won't make it uglier than it has already become."

His feet dragged under the weight of his heart as he ap-

proached her. "*B'Ellahi*...you loved me.... You said so....
I *felt* it."

"Whatever I said, whatever you think you felt, it's over.
I never want to see you again."

He caught her, the feel of her intensifying his desperation. "You might think you mean it now, but you're mine,
Jala. And no matter how long it takes, I swear to you, I
will reclaim you. I will make you beg to be mine again."

"I was never yours. If you think you have a claim on
me, I *will* repay you for saving my life one day. But not
with my life."

His fingers sank into her shoulders, as if it would stop
her from vanishing. "I don't care who Najeeb is. I'll destroy him before I let him have you. I'll destroy anyone
who comes near you."

The disdain in her eyes rose. Everything he said sent
her another step beyond retrieval.

"So now I know why you're called *Al Moddammer*."
The Destroyer. The label he'd earned when he'd decimated
conspiracies and terrorist organizations. "You annihilate
anyone who becomes an obstacle to your objectives. Not
to mention anyone who comes close to *you*."

His heart seized painfully. He'd never thought she'd
ever use *that* knowledge against him. What else had he
been wrong about?

Her disgust as she severed his convulsive grip told
him this was it. It was over. Worse still, it might never
have been real. Everything they'd shared, everything he'd
thought they'd meant to each other might have all been in
his mind.

Before she receded out of his life, she murmured, "Find
yourself someone else who might have a death wish. Because I don't."

One

Present day...

"Do you have a death wish?"

Mohab almost laughed out loud. A bitterly amused huff did escape him as he rose to his feet to meet the king of Judar.

What were the odds? That these exact words would be the first thing Kamal Aal Masood said to him when they'd been the last thing the man's kid sister had flung at Mohab?

Guess it *was* true what was said about Kamal and Jala. That the two youngest in the Aal Masood sibling quartet could have been identical twins—if they hadn't been born male and female and twelve years apart. Their resemblance *was* uncanny.

With the historical enmity between their kingdoms, Mohab had only seen Kamal from afar. He'd last beheld him at the time of his *joloos*—as he'd sat on the throne, five and a half years ago. Not that Mohab had manipulated his way into Judar that night to see him. Jala had been his only objective. But *she* hadn't attended her own brother's wedding. Yet another thing he'd failed to predict where she was concerned.

Something else he'd failed to predict was how it would feel seeing this guy up close. Kamal looked so much like Jala, it…ached deep in his chest.

It was as if someone had taken Jala and turned her into an older, intimidating male version of herself. They shared the same wealth of raven hair, the same whiskey-colored eyes and the same bone structure. The only differences were those of gender. Kamal's bronze complexion was shades darker than Jala's golden flawlessness, and at six foot six, the king of Judar would tower over his sister's statuesque five-nine, just as *he* once had. Her big brother was also more than double her size, but they shared the same feline grace and perfect proportions. While all that made her the embodiment of a fairy-tale princess, Kamal was the epitome of a hardened desert raider, exuding limitless power. And exercising it, too.

At forty, Kamal was one of the most influential individuals in the world, and had been so even before his two older brothers had abdicated the throne of Judar to him in a chain reaction of court drama and royal family scandals that still rocked the region and changed its course forever.

Now Kamal's lupine eyes simmered with the trademark menace famous for intimidating anyone he seared with his gaze. "Anything you find particularly amusing, Aal Ghaanem?"

"Your opening remark revived a memory of another… person mentioning death wishes." At Kamal's fierce glower, Mohab's smile spread. "What? You think I find you, or being escorted here like a prisoner of war, amusing?"

He'd expected worse arriving in Judar, with tensions

between Saraya and Judar at a historic high. In fact, just yesterday, his king had all but declared war on Judar during a global broadcast from a UN summit. For Mohab, a prince of Saraya second in rank only to the king and his heirs, to land uninvited on Judarian soil in these fraught times was cause for extreme concern. Especially when said prince also happened to be the former head of Saraya's secret service. He'd expected to be put on the first flight out of Judar. Or even to be taken into custody.

In a preemptive bluff, he'd asserted he had time-sensitive business with King Kamal and the king would punish whoever detained him. That sent border security officials at the airport scrambling for orders from the royal palace. Mohab had half expected his gamble to fall through, that Kamal would have him kicked out of the kingdom. But within minutes, a dozen of Judar's finest secret-service men had descended on Mohab, breathing down his neck all the way here.

Apparently they considered him that dangerous. He was flattered, really.

"So you find death wishes a source of amusement? A daredevil by nature, not only by trade, eh? Figures. But aren't you also supposed to be meticulous and prudent? I thought that's why you're still in one piece after all the crazy stunts you've pulled. Isn't it the first thing you're taught when you're hatched in Saraya—that Judar doesn't sustain life for your species?"

His species. The Aal Ghaanems. The Aal Masoods' mortal enemies. *Aih.* There was *that* stumbling block, too.

"So again…*do* you have a death wish? Don't you know that, now more than ever, a high-profile Sarayan like you at large in Judar could have been targeted for any level of retribution?"

Mohab flattened a palm over his heart. "I'm touched you're concerned about keeping me in one piece. But I assure you, I behaved in an exemplary fashion, antagonizing no one."

"No one but me. Arriving unannounced, terrorizing my subjects, forcing me to drop everything to investigate your incursion. Is this your king's last hope now that he's put his foot in his mouth on global feed? Is he afraid I'll finally knock him off his throne, as I should have long ago? Has he sent his wild card to deal with the crisis…at the root?"

"You think I'm here to…what? Assassinate you?" A huff of incredulity burst from Mohab. "I may be into impossible missions, but I'm not fond of suicidal ones. And I was almost strip-searched for anything that could even make you sneeze."

Kamal's laserlike gaze contemplated Mohab's mocking grin. "From my reports, you can probably take out my royal guard stripped and with both hands tied behind your back."

"Ah, you flatter me, King Kamal. I'd need one hand to go through them all."

The other man's steady gaze told him Kamal believed Mohab was capable of just that—and more—and wasn't the least bit fooled by his joking tone. "I have records of some true mission-impossible scenarios that you've pulled off. If anyone can enter a maximum-security palace with only the clothes on his back and manage to blow it up and walk away without a scratch, it's you."

Mohab's lips twitched. "If you believe I can get away with your murder, why did you agree to see me?"

"Because I'm intrigued."

"Enough to risk letting such a lethal entity within reach? You must be bored out of your mind being king."

Kamal exhaled. "You don't know the half of it—or how good *you* have it. A prince who is in no danger of finding himself on a throne, a black-ops professional who had the luxury of switching to a freelance career…emphasis on the 'free' part."

"While *you're* the king of a minor kingdom you've made into a major one, and a revered leader who has limitless power at his fingertips and the most amazing family a man can dream of having."

"Apart from my incomparable wife and children, I'd switch places with you in a heartbeat."

Mohab laughed out loud. "The last thing I expected coming here is that I'd be standing with you, in the heart of Aal Masood territory, with us envying each other."

"In a better world, I would have offered you anything to have your skills at my disposal and you at my side. Too bad we're on opposite sides with no way to bridge the divide."

Mohab pounced on the opening. "That's why I'm here. To offer not only to bridge that divide, but to obliterate it."

Kamal frowned. "You deal in extractions, containments and cleanups. Why send you to offer political solutions?"

"I'm here on my own initiative because *I'm* the solution."

His declaration was met by an empty stare.

Then Kamal drawled, "Strange. You seem quite solid." Mohab chuckled at Kamal's unexpected dry-as-tinder wit, drawing a rumble from Kamal. "I have zero tolerance for wastes of time. If you prove to be one, you will spend a few nights as an honored guest in my personal dungeon."

"Is this a way to talk to the man who can give you Jareer?"

Kamal clamped his arm. "*Kaffa monawaraat wa ghomood*…enough evasions and ambiguity. Explain, and fast, or…"

"Put down your threats. I *am* here to mend our kingdoms' relations, and there's nothing I want more than to accomplish that as fast as possible."

"*Zain.* You have ten minutes."

"Twenty." Before Kamal blasted him, Mohab preempted him. "*Don't* say fifteen."

Kamal's gaze lengthened. "As an only child you missed out on having an older sibling kick your ass in your formative years. I'm close to rectifying your deficiency."

Mohab grinned. "Think you can take me on, King Kamal?"

"Definitely."

And Mohab believed it. Kamal wasn't a pampered royal depending on others' service and protection. This man was a warrior first and foremost. That he'd chosen to fight in the boardroom and now in the world's political arenas didn't mean he wouldn't be as effective on an actual battlefield.

Before Mohab made a rejoinder, the king turned and crossed his expansive stateroom to the sitting area. Mohab suspected it was to hide a smile so as not to acknowledge this affinity that had sprung up between them.

Kamal resumed speaking as soon as Mohab took a seat across from him. "So why do you think *you* can give me Jareer...when I already have it, Sheikh Prince Solution?"

A laugh burst out of Mohab's depths. That clinched it. He didn't care that other people thought Kamal scary or boorish. To him, the guy was just plain rocking fun.

Kamal's lips twisted in response, but didn't lift.

"There is no law prohibiting an Aal Masood from smiling at an Aal Ghaanem, you know."

Kamal's lips pursed instead. "I may issue one prohibiting just that. The way you're going, you might end up making the dispute between Judar and Saraya even more... insoluble."

Mohab sighed. "So...Jareer, euphemistically referred to as our kingdoms' *contested region*..."

"*And* currently known as our kingdoms' *future war zone,*" Kamal finished.

Not if Mohab managed to resolve this.

Jareer used to be under Saraya's rule. But the past few Sarayan monarchs had had no foresight. They'd centralized everything, neglecting then abandoning outlying regions. Jareer, on the border with Judar, had always been considered useless, because it lacked resources, and traitorous, because its citizens were akin to "enemy sympathizers." So when Judar had laid claim to Jareer, with its people's welcome, Mohab's grandfather, King Othman, had considered it good riddance.

But when Mohab's uncle, King Hassan, sat on Saraya's throne, he'd reignited old conflicts with Judar. His favorite crusade had been reclaiming Jareer. Not because he'd suspected its future importance, but to spite the region's inhabitants—and because he wanted more reasons to fight the Aal Masoods.

Then, two months ago, oil had been discovered in Jareer. Now the situation had evolved from an idle conflict between two monarchs to a struggle over limitless wealth and power. In a war between the two kingdoms, Saraya would be decimated for generations to come.

Only Mohab had the power to stop this catastrophe. Theoretically. There was still the possibility that Kamal would hear his proposition and reward his audacity by throwing him in that personal dungeon before wiping Saraya off the face of the earth.

One thing made Mohab hope this wouldn't happen. Kamal himself. He was convinced that, though Kamal had every reason to crush Saraya, he would rather not. He hadn't become one of the greatest kings by being reactionary—or by achieving prosperity for his kingdom at the cost of another kingdom's destruction.

At least, Mohab hoped he was right. He *had* read Kamal's "twin" all wrong once before after all....

"I will be disappointed if, after all this staring at me, you can't draw me from memory."

Jarred out of his thoughts by Kamal's drawl, Mohab blinked at him. "You just remind me of someone so much, it keeps sidetracking me."

"The same someone who made the death wish comment, eh?"

Not only brilliant, but intuitive, too. Mohab nodded.

"And there I was under the impression I was unique."

Mohab sighed. "You are…both of you. Two of a kind."

Kamal sat forward, ire barely contained. "As charmed as I am by all this…*nostalgia* of yours, I have a date with my wife in an hour, and I'd rather be late for my own funeral than for her. I might make you early for yours if you don't talk. Fast."

"All right. I am the rightful heir to Jareer."

Kamal's eyebrows shot up. He hadn't seen this coming. No one could have.

Mohab explained. "For centuries, Jareer was an independent land, and my mother's tribe, the Aal Kussaimis, ruled it up till a hundred and fifty years ago. But with my great-great-grandmother marrying an Aal Ghaanem, a treaty was struck with Saraya to annex the region, with terms for autonomy while under Sarayan rule and with provisions for secession if those terms weren't observed.

"When Jareer found itself on its own again under my grandfather's rule, it saw no reason to enforce the secession rules, as it was effectively separated from Saraya anyway. Then Judar offered its protection. But in truth, Jareer belongs to neither Judar nor Saraya. It belongs to my maternal tribe. I would have brought you the records of our claim for as far back as a thousand years, but after yesterday's fiasco, I had to rush to intervene before I could get everything ready. However, rest assured, the claim is heavily documented by the tribe's elders and historians."

Kamal blinked as if emerging from a trance. "That's your solution? Inserting the Aal Kussaimis as preceding claimants? Widening the dispute and adding more fuel to the fire?"

"Actually, I am ending the dispute. The Aal Kussaimis' claim trumps both the Aal Ghaanems' and the Aal Masoods'. Any regional or international court would sanction that claim."

Kamal's eyes burned with contemplation. "If all this is true, shouldn't I be talking to the tribe's elder? Who can't be you since you're…how old? Thirty?"

"Thirty-eight. But while it's true I'm not the tribe's elder, I am the highest-ranking tribe member by merit. I was elected the tribe's leader years ago. Which effectively makes me the king of Jareer."

Kamal's lashes lowered. A testament to his surprise.

When his gaze rose again, it was tranquil. That didn't fool Mohab for a second. He could almost hear the gears of Kamal's formidable mind screeching.

"Interesting. So you're claiming to be *King* Solution. Even if you prove to be the first, how do you propose to be the second?"

"Proving my claim is a foregone conclusion. The second should be self-evident."

"Not to me."

Jala's exact words that fateful night. Said in the same tone. Kamal's likeness to her had suddenly ceased to be reminiscent and had become only grating.

Mohab gritted his teeth. "My uncle assumed I would never invoke my claim, that I would always let him speak for me concerning Jareer's fate. And he was right—I didn't have time to be more than an honorary leader and had no desire to upset a status quo my people were perfectly content with under Judar's protection. But now things have changed."

Kamal huffed. "Tell me about it. Just two months ago, you were the 'rightful heir' to a stretch of desert with three towns and seven villages whose people lived on date and Arabian coffee production, souvenir manufacturing and desert tourism. Now you're the king of a land sitting on top of one of the biggest oil reservoirs ever discovered."

"I have no personal stake in Jareer's newfound wealth. I'm not interested in being richer, and I never wanted to be king. However, my people are demanding I declare Jareer an independent state and that I become their full-fledged ruler. But business and politics aren't my forte. So while I will do my people's bidding, I think it's in their best interests to leave their new oil-based prosperity to the experts."

"By experts, I assume you mean oil moguls."

"With you in charge of every step they take into Jareer."

Kamal raised one eyebrow. "You want me to run the show?"

"Yes."

Kamal digested this. "So that's Judar and Jareer and the oil companies. What about Saraya?"

"As a Sarayan, too, and because I admit the treaties with Saraya were never properly resolved before entering into the new ones with Judar, I will recognize its claim."

"So you claim Jareer, and split the cake between us all. Why do you assume I'll consider it? If I can have the whole cake?"

He sat forward, holding Kamal's gaze. "I do because you're an honorable man and a just king. Because I believe you'll do everything in your power to avoid escalating hostilities between our kingdoms. Before, it was about family feuds and pride. Now we're talking staggering wealth and power. If you decimate my claim and take all of Jareer, those who stand to lose that much would cause unspeakable damage. I regularly deal with situations that rage over way less, and believe me, nothing is worth the price of such conflicts."

"So how do you propose we split the cake?"

"For its historical role and ties to Jareer, and because both Judar and Jareer will need its cooperation, Saraya will get twenty percent of Jareer's oil. In recognition of Judar's more recent claim and its much bigger role in Jareer till this day, Judar gets forty percent. Jareer gets the other forty percent. Plus, its inhabitants would be first in line for all benefits and job opportunities that arise, and you will also be responsible to provide training for them."

"You've got it all worked out, don't you?"

"I have been working on my pitch since the oil's discovery. I was far from ready, but my uncle's theatrics at the UN yesterday forced my hand prematurely."

"What if I don't like your percentages or terms?"

"I would grant you whatever you wish."

"Even if you wanted to, as kings, we're not omnipotent. Why would your people agree to let you be so generous with their resources?"

Here it was. Moment of truth. The point of all this.

He took the plunge. "They would because it would be the *mahr* of your sister, Princess Jala."

Kamal rose to his feet in perfect calmness. It screamed instantaneous rejection more than anything openly indignant would have.

"No."

The cold, final word fell on Mohab like a lash. As Jala's rejection once had.

He resisted the urge to flinch at the sting. "Just no?"

"Consider yourself honored I deemed to articulate it. That you dared to voice this boggles the mind."

"Why?"

Kamal glared down at him. "I'll have my secretary of state draw you up an inventory of the reasons."

"Give me the broad lines."

"How about just one? Your bloodline."

"You'd condemn a man by others' transgressions?"

"We do inherit others' mistakes and enmities."

"And we can resolve them, not insist on regurgitating hatreds and spawning warring generations."

"The Aal Masoods aren't angels, but there is good reason why we abhor you, why all attempts at peacemaking fell through for centuries. Surely you remember the last marriage between our kingdoms and what your great-grandfather did to my great-aunt. I'm not letting my sister marry a man who comes from a family where the men mistreat their women."

"My great-grandfather and uncle don't represent the rest of us. *I* am nothing like them. You can investigate me further. And then consider the merits of my proposal. Once I claim Jareer, my uncle can retreat from his warpath. We'd appease his pride while going over his head in forging peaceful relations between all sides, to the benefit of all our people." Mohab rose to his feet to face him. "What I'm proposing is the best solution for all concerned, now and into the far future. And you know it."

After a protracted stare, Kamal finally exhaled. "We can forge peace with other kinds of treaties. Why bring marriage into this? And more important, why Jala? If you want to solidify the new alliance in the oldest way in the book, and the most enduring in our region, the Aal Masoods have other princesses who would definitely be more acceptable to your stick-in-the-mud family."

"My family has nothing to do with it. Jala is *my* choice." Kamal's astonishment made Mohab decide to come clean, as much as it was prudent to. "I had a…thing for Jala years ago, and I thought she reciprocated. It didn't end as I hoped. Now, years later, with both of us still unattached, I thought it might be fate's way of telling me I had to make another attempt at claiming the one woman who captured my fancy…and wouldn't let go. So while resolving our kingdoms' long-standing conflicts would certainly be a bonus, she's always been my main objective."

Expecting Kamal, as Jala's brother, to be offended—or at least to grill him about the nature of the "thing" he'd had for Jala—Kamal surprised him again, a hint of a smile dawning. "You mean discovering oil in Jareer and the crisis that ensued just presented you with the best bargaining chip to propose? And you didn't propose before because you never had enough leverage?"

Mohab shrugged, tension killing him. "Do I have enough now?"

Kamal's smile became definite. "If I disregard the stench of your paternal lineage and consider you based on your own merits, this might be a good idea. A perfect one, even. Knowing Jala, she'd never marry of her own accord and I hate to think she'll end up alone. And you, apart from the despicable flaw of having the Aal Ghaanem blood and name, seem like a…reasonably good match for her."

"So you're saying yes?"

"A yes isn't mine to say. I can't force her to marry you and wouldn't even if I could. Clearly this marriage quest of yours is hardly a done deal, since you require my intervention to even reach her. I won't ask what earned you a place on Jala's viciously strict no-approach list. *Ullah* knows I'm the last man to go all holier-than-thou on you for whatever transgression you committed to deserve this kind of treatment."

What would Kamal say if Mohab told him he didn't know exactly why he'd deserved that till this day?

Kamal gazed into the distance as if peering into a distasteful past. "I once did unforgivable things to the one woman who'd captured *my* fancy and wouldn't let go, and it took the intervention of others to give me that second chance with her."

"So you're paying it forward."

Kamal's eyes returned to his, the crooked smile back. "I am. *But* if she agrees to marry you, I'll take *sixty* percent as her *mahr*. If she refuses, the whole deal is off—and we'll draw up another treaty that saves your king's face so he can go sit in his throne and stop throwing war-agitating tantrums."

Mohab's first impulse was to kiss Kamal on both cheeks. This was beyond anything he'd come here expecting.

He extended his hand to Kamal instead, his smile the widest it had been in…six years. "Deal. You won't regret this."

Kamal shook his hand slowly. "You were wrong when you said you don't know much about business. You know nothing. You could have gotten me to agree to thirty percent. You're holding all the cards after all."

Mohab's smiled widened more. "I'm not so oblivious that I don't know the power I wield. But I would never haggle over Jala's *mahr*. If my decision didn't affect millions of people in both Saraya and Jareer, I would have given you the whole thing."

"You got it that bad?" Kamal drilled him with an incredulous gaze. "Do you *love* her?"

Love? He once had…or thought he had. But now he knew it hadn't been real. Because nothing real could ever exist for a man like him. He only knew he couldn't move on. And that she hadn't moved on, either. He was still obsessed with their every touch, had starved for her every pleasure. Love didn't enter into the equation. Not only was it an illusion, it was one he couldn't afford.

But the pact he'd struck with Kamal was real. As was

his hunger for Jala. That was more than enough. In fact, that was everything.

Kamal waved his hand. "Don't answer that. I don't think you *can* answer. If you haven't seen her in years, whatever you felt for her back then might be totally moot once you come face-to-face with each other again. So I won't hold you to this proposal for now. But since Jala is the most intractable entity I have the misfortune to know and love…" At Mohab's raised eyebrow, Kamal sighed. "*Aih,* she takes after her older brother, as Aliyah tells me."

Mohab did a double take. It was amazing, the change that came over Kamal's face as he mentioned his wife and queen. It was as if he glowed inside just thinking of her.

Kamal went on. "But for this to have a prayer of working, I need to give you much more of a helping hand than putting you in the same room with her. I need to give *her* a shove. I'll make it sound as if refusal isn't an option. Of course, if she *really* wants to refuse, she will, no matter what." His lips spread into a smile again. "All I can hope is that if I make things sound drastic enough, it'll give you that chance to make your approach. The rest… is up to you."

Two

"You...*what?*"

Jala stared at Kamal, her shrill cry ringing in her own ears.

Staggering, she collapsed on the nearest horizontal surface, gaping up at Kamal who came to stand over her.

"I lied."

Ya Ullah. She *had* heard right the first time.

Another cry of sheer incredulity scratched her throat raw. "How could you do this to me? Are you *insane?*"

Kamal shrugged, not looking in the least repentant. "I had to get you here. Sorry."

"*Sorry?* You let me have a thousand panic attacks during the hours it took me to get here, thinking that Farooq was lying in hospital, critically injured, and you say... sorry?"

Even now that she knew Farooq was safe, the horror still reverberated in her bones. She'd never known such desperation, not even when she'd been held hostage and thought she'd die a violent death.

Fury seethed inside of her. "Don't you know what you did to me? As I thought of beautiful, vital Farooq lying broken, struggling for his life, how I wept as I thought how much he had to live for, as I thought of Carmen losing her soul mate, of Mennah growing up without her father.... You're a monstrous *pig,* Kamal!"

Kamal winced. "I said he was injured but that he was stable. I wanted you here, but didn't want to scare you more than necessary. How am I responsible for your exaggerations?"

"How? *How?*" She threw her hands up in the air in frustration. "How does Aliyah *bear* you?"

Kamal had the temerity to flash her that wolfish grin of his. "I never ask. I just wallow in the miracle of her, and that she thinks I'm the best thing that ever walked the earth."

"Then Aliyah, although she *looks* sane, is clearly deranged. Or under a spell...."

"It's called love." Kamal raised his hands before she exploded again. "I *am* sorry. But you said you'd never set foot here again, and I knew you wouldn't come unless you thought one of us was dying."

"I know you're ruthless and manipulative and a dozen other inhuman adjectives but...argh! Whatever you needed to drag me here for, you could have tried telling me the truth first!"

Kamal smirked. "*Aih,* and when that didn't work, I would have tried the lie next. I *would* have ordered you to come, but knowing you, you would have probably renounced your Judarian citizenship just so I'd stop being your king. If you weren't that intractable I wouldn't have had to lie, and you wouldn't have had those harrowing sixteen hours."

"So it's now my fault? You—you humongous, malignant rat! What could possibly be enough reason for you to drag me back here with this terrible lie?"

"Just that Judar is about to go to war."

She shot back up to her feet. "*Kaffa,* Kamal…enough. I'm already here. So stop *lying.*"

His face was suddenly grim. "No lie this time." He put his hand on her shoulder, gently pressed her down to the couch, coming down beside her this time. "It's a long story."

She gaped at him as he recounted it, plunging deeper into a surreal scape with every word.

But wars did erupt over far less, especially in their region. This was real.

When he was done, she exhaled. "You can't even consider war over oil rights, no matter how massive. Aren't you the wizard of diplomacy who peacefully resolves conflicts to every side's benefit?"

"Seems you're not familiar with King Hassan." A scoff almost escaped her. Oh, she was *so* very familiar with King Hassan. "Some people are immune to diplomacy."

"And *you're* not posturing and allowing your council to egg you on with hand-me-down rivalries and vendettas?"

It was Kamal's turn to scoff. "Give me some credit, Jala. I care nothing about any of this bull. *I* don't have an inflamed ego and don't borrow others' enmities."

"Yet you're letting someone who has and does drag you down to his level, when you should contain him and his petty aggressions." She exhaled her exasperation. "No wonder I did everything I could to get out of this godforsaken region and had to be told my oldest brother was dying to set foot here again. All this feudal backwardness is just…nauseating. You'd think nothing ever changed since the eleventh century!"

"War over oil rights is *very* twenty-first century."

"Congratulations to all of you, then, for your leap into modern warfare. I hope you'll enjoy deploying long-range missiles and playing high-tech war games." She muttered something about monkeys under her breath. "I still don't get why you conned me back here. You want me to have a front row seat with you lunkheads when the war begins?"

He reached for her hand, his eyes cajoling. Uh-oh.

"You actually play the lead role in averting this catastrophe."

"What could I possibly have to do with resolving your political conflicts?"

"Everything really. Only you can stop the war now, by marrying an Aal Ghaanem prince."

"What?"

"Only a blood-mixing union will end hostilities and forge a long-lasting alliance."

She snatched her hand from his grasp, erupting to her feet. "Did I say you were stuck in the eleventh century? You've just stumbled five more centuries backward. *Not* so good seeing you, Kamal. And don't expect to lay eyes on me for a long while. Certainly never in Judar again."

Kamal gave her that unfazed glance that made her want to shriek at the top of her lungs. "It's this or war. The war you know full well would come at an unthinkable price to everyone in Judar—and in Saraya and Jareer, too."

Wincing at the terrible images his words smeared across her imagination, she gritted out, "Let's say for argument's sake that I don't think you're all insane to be still dabbling in marriages of state to settle political disputes. The Aal Masoods have many princesses who're just right for the role of political bride. In fact, some have been born and bred for the role. So how are any of you foolish enough to consider *me*—aka the Prodigal Princess?"

Lethal steel came into Kamal's eyes. "Others' opinions are irrelevant. You're *the* princess of Judar. Only your blood could end centuries of enmity and forge an unbreakable alliance. So it's not a choice. You are getting married to the Aal Ghaanem prince."

"Wow. If you wore a crown, I'd think it got too tight on your swelling head and gave you brain damage. Anyway, if you think you can sacrifice me at the altar of your tribal reconciliations, you're suffering from serious delusions."

"We all offer sacrifices when our kingdom needs us."

"What sacrifices?" She coughed a furious chuckle. "To remain married to Carmen, Farooq tossed his crownprince rank to Shehab when our kingdom needed him. Shehab did the same with you, to marry Farah. You grabbed the rank and *sacrifice* only because it got you Aliyah in the bargain. You're all living in ecstatic-ever-afters because you did exactly what you wanted and never sacrificed a thing for 'our kingdom.'"

"Farooq and Shehab had the option of passing on their duty. I didn't, like you don't now. And I thought it *was* a sacrifice when I accepted my duty."

"No, you didn't. You knew nothing less than another threat of war would get Aliyah to say good-morning to you again. You pounced on the 'duty' that would make her your queen and pretended to hate your 'fate.'" At his raised eyebrows, she smirked. "I can figure things out pretty good, *ya akhi al azeez*. So spare me the sacrifice speech, brother dear. You're out of your mind if you think you can sway me into this by appealing to my patriotism."

"Then it will be your steep humanitarian inclinations. You've been in war zones. You know that once war starts, there's no stopping the chain reaction that harvests lives in its path. As a woman who lives to alleviate the suffering of others, and who can stop this nightmarish scenario, you'll do anything to abort it, even if you abhor Judar and the whole region. And the very idea of marriage."

The terrible knowledge that he was right, if there was

no other choice, seeped into her marrow. "So now what? You'll line up Aal Ghaanem princes and I'll pick the least offensive one? And the one I pick would just accept being sacrificed for his kingdom's peace and prosperity?"

"If a man considers marrying you a sacrifice, he must be devoid of even a drop of testosterone."

"You won't appeal to my feminine ego, either. Any man in the region would rather jump out of a ten-story window than marry a woman like me, *the* princess of Judar or not."

"A woman like you would be an irreplaceable treasure to any man in any region."

"Blatant brotherly hyperbole aside, no, *a woman like me* wouldn't. A woman living alone in the West since she was eighteen is the stuff of region-wide dishonor around here. It had to be something as dire as the threat of war and the promise of unending oil to sweeten my scandalous pill for one of those stuck-in-the-dark-ages princes."

"The new generation of princes are nowhere as bad as that."

"The only one I know who isn't is Najeeb. But I bet *he* won't be joining the lineup." Her lips twisted with remembered bitterness. "King Hassan would never sacrifice his heir to such a fate as me, no matter the incentives."

Kamal waved his hand. "You won't suffer the discomfort of a lineup. The Aal Ghaanem prince has already been chosen."

She almost had to pick her jaw off the floor this time. "How can I express my gratitude that you've gone the extra mile and abolished whatever choice I had in this antiquated process?"

Kamal's lips twitched. "Let me rephrase my extremely misleading statement. The Aal Ghaanem prince volunteered. And he is already here. But he had the consideration to let me prepare you before he came in. So shall I send him in…or do you need some more time before you meet your groom-to-be?"

She sank back onto the couch, objections and insults swarming so violently it was impossible to pick one to voice.

Calmly disregarding her apoplectic state, Kamal bent and kissed her cheek. "Give this a chance, and it'll all work out for the best. You have me as the best example for *assa ann takraho shai'an wa hwa khairon lakkom*."

You may hate something and it's for your best.

Before she could do something drastic, like poke him in the eye, he straightened, turned on his heel and walked away.

She watched him disappear, all her mental functions on the fritz.

What had just happened?

Was she really back in Judar? Only to find herself being pushed into a far worse cage than anything her previous life here had been? Could it be true that refusal wasn't an option?

Suddenly a suspicion cleaved into her brain.

The logical progression to this nightmare.

The identity of this "volunteer."

The man who was the reason she'd sworn never to return to this region. He *was* an Aal Ghaanem prince, even if the world forgot that most of the time.

But he would never volunteer to…to…

You're mine, Jala. And no matter how long it takes, I swear to you, I will reclaim you. I will make you beg to be mine again.

The promise…the *threat*…that had circulated in her being for six long years, burning her to the core with its malicious arrogance and possessiveness, reverberated in her bones.

No. He'd just said that out of spite, to poison whatever

reprieve walking away would grant her. He hadn't really wanted to reclaim her. Not when he'd only claimed her as a means to an end. An end he must believe he'd long achieved....

Her heart kicked, had her pitching forward to the edge of her seat. The door of the reception room was opening.

The next moment, her heart battered her ribs. Time ceased. Reality fell away. Everything converged on one thing. The shadow separating from the darkness. A shape she remembered all too well.

Him.

No. *No.* Not when she'd finally managed to purge his malignant memory. She must stop this confrontation from coming to pass, flee...*now.*

She didn't move. Couldn't. Could only sit there, her every nerve unraveling as soundless steps brought him into the circle of light where she sat exposed, besieged.

His eyes were the first things that emerged out of the gloom. Those fire pits had haunted her dreams and tormented her waking hours since she'd last seen them.

But the tremors arcing through her weren't from what she saw in them, or the blow of his presence or its implications. It was the awareness that had swept her from the first moment she'd ever encountered him. Even amidst the terror of the hostage crisis, it had yanked her out of reality, plunged her into a stunned free fall where only he existed. For that same feeling to mushroom again now, after all that had happened...

He blinked, and the vice garroting her snapped, propelling her to her feet and to the French windows.

Her steps picked up speed as her exit to the palace gardens neared...then it disappeared. Behind a wall of muscle and maleness. It was as if he'd materialized in her path.

He didn't try to detain her, didn't need to. His very aura snared her. And that was before her gaze streaked up, found him looking at her with that trance-inducing intensity.

Finding him so near, after all these years, after what he'd cost her....

Her grip on consciousness softened. The world swirled as she stared up at him, a prisoner to her own enervation. And again the sheer injustice of it all hit her.

No one should be endowed with all this. He was too... everything. And even in the subdued lighting and through the veil of her own wavering senses she could see he was even more than she remembered. Six years had taken him from the epitome of manhood to godlike levels.

He towered over her, even though she was six feet in her heels, his physique that of an Olympian, his face that of an avenging angel, every inch of him composed of planes and hollows and slashes of power and perfection. Adding to his lethal assets, his wealth of sun-gilded mahogany hair was now long enough to be gathered at his nape, the severe scrape emphasizing the ruggedness of his leonine forehead and the vigor of his hairline. A trim new beard and mustache accentuated the jut of his cheekbones and the dominance of his jawline and completed the ruthless desert raider image. Maturity had added more of everything to that supreme being of bronze and steel who'd taken her breath away and had held it out of reach for as long as he'd had her under his spell. Something she'd thought she'd broken.

But if, after all she'd been through, all the maturation she'd thought she'd undergone, he could still look at her and take control of her senses, then the spell couldn't *be* broken.

But this unadulterated coveting in his eyes... She couldn't be reading it right.

Still, when he took a step closer, he vibrated with something that simulated barely checked hunger. Which would be unleashed at the slightest provocation—a word, a gasp....

But she was incapable of even those. She'd expended all her power in her escape effort. Now she was caught in stasis, waiting for his next move to reanimate her.

None came. He stared down at her, as if her nearness affected him just as acutely. When *he'd* been the one who'd planned this ambush, who'd been lying in wait for her.

The barricades around her resentment melted, shattering her inertia, imbuing her limbs with the steadiness of outrage as she put the distance he'd obliterated back between them.

"Guess your memory must be patchy from all the head blows I hear is an occupational hazard in your line of work. Your presence can only be explained by partial to total amnesia."

Another blink lowered his thick, gold-tipped lashes, eclipsing the infernos of his eyes and his reaction. Then they swept up, exposing her to a different kind of heat. Surprise? Challenge? Humor?

Just the idea that it could be the latter poured acid on her inflamed nerves. "Let me fill one paramount hole in your recollections. What I last said to you remains in full force now. I never want to see you again. So you can take whatever game you think you're playing and go straight to hell."

She swept around then, desperation to get away from him fueling her steps...and her arm was snagged in a hard, warm grip.

Before she could fully register the bolt that zapped her, a tug swirled her around smoothly, as if in a choreographed dance, and brought her slamming against him from breast to calf.

Before she could draw another breath, one of his hands slipped into the hair at her nape, immobilizing her head and tilting her face upward. The other hand trailed a heavy path of possession down to her buttocks. Then, as he held her prisoner, exerting no force but that of his will, he let her see it. The very thing she'd once reveled in experiencing—the lethal beast he kept hidden under the civilized veneer. Its cunning savagery had assured his survival in the dangerous existence he'd chosen, his triumph over the most deadly enemies. That beast appeared to be starving—and she was what would sate its cravings.

Holding her stunned gaze, his own crackling with a dizzying mixture of calculation and lust, he lowered his head.

Feeling she'd disintegrate at the touch of his lips, she averted her face at the last moment.

His lips landed at the corner of her mouth, plucking convulsively at her flesh. The familiarity of his lips, the unfamiliarity of his facial hair, sparked each nerve ending individually. The gusts of his breath filled her with his scent, burying her under an avalanche of memory. Of how it used to feel to lose herself to the ecstasy of his powerful possession.

The hand on her buttocks pressed her closer, letting her feel his arousal, wringing hers from her depths. Before she could deal with this blow, the hand holding her head combed through her hair. Each stroke sent delight cascading from every hair root, spilled moans from her depths in answer to the unintelligible bass murmurings from him. Then his other hand caressed its way beneath her jacket, freeing her blouse from her skirt…and delving below.

A gasp tore out of her as those calloused fingers splayed against her sizzling flesh, imprinting it like a brand, making her instinctively press closer. And then he took his onslaught to the next level.

Yanking up her skirt, he slipped below her panties to cup her buttocks, kneading her taut flesh hungrily before hauling her against him. Weightless, in his power, she keened as the long-craved steel of his erection ground against her core. A scalding growl rolled in his gut as he tugged one thigh, opening her around his hips, spreading her for his domination, while the hand at her back plastered her heaving chest against his. Her breasts swelled with each rub against his hard power, the abrasion of their clothes turning her nipples to pinpoints of agony.

She writhed in his hold as he singed kisses down her neck, ravaged her in suckles that would mark her skin, sending vicious pleasure hurtling through her blood, lodging into her womb with each savage pull.

All existence converged on him, became him—his body and breath, his taste and feel, his hands and mouth—as he strummed her flesh, reclaimed her every inch and response. With just a touch, she'd ceased to be herself, becoming a mass of need wrapped around him, open to him, his to exploit and plunder…to pleasure and possess.

She could no longer hear anything but her thundering heart and their strident breathing as he raised her up and slid her down his body in leisurely excursions. He had her riding his erection through their clothes. He dipped his head to capture her nipple through her bra in massaging nips, sending never-forgotten ecstasy corkscrewing through her every nerve ending.

Her moans droned, interrupted only by sharp intakes of breath. The flowing throb between her thighs escalated into pounding, tipping from discomfort into pain until she cried out. At her distressed if unmistakable demand, he shuddered beneath her, snapping his head up. Then, eyes glazed with ferocity, he crashed his lips onto her wide-open mouth and thrust deep.

She plunged into his taste, fierce wonder spreading in her flickering awareness. How did she remember it so accurately, crave it so acutely still?

Then everything ceased as his tongue invaded her, commanded hers to tangle and duel and drink deeper from the well of passion she'd once drowned in.

Then something stirred in her, shutting down her mind; something cold and ugly tore through the delirium. A realization.

This had happened before. This had been what he'd done to her that last time. He'd taken over her senses, exploited her responses, inundated her with physical satisfaction… and almost decimated her soul and psyche in the process.

Now he'd taken her over again, as if a mountain of pain and resentment didn't exist between them. She was letting him pull her strings again when he only ever saw her as a means to an end. Having an even bigger end this time, he'd decided to go into all-out invasion mode from the get-go. And she was letting him. *No.*

Anger and humiliation shattered the spell, had her struggling in his arms as if fighting for her life.

Stiffening for a long moment, as if unable to make up his mind whether that was an attempt to get away or to press closer, he finally tore his lips from hers and slid her down his body and back to the ground.

Every muscle burning from the slow poison of need with which he'd reinfected her, she staggered, groping for equilibrium. She'd taken barely a step away when his hands descended on her shoulders and pulled her back against him.

She couldn't even tremble, the control she'd long struggled for shattered, leaving her drained. She could only lean back against him limply, her head rolling on his shoulder.

Taking this as consent, he cupped her breasts, pressing against her as he groaned in her ear. "I didn't intend to do this. I still have no control over what I'm doing right this second. I walked in here and it was as if time hit Rewind, as if we'd never been apart. And just like you always do, you overrode my every rational thought and impulse with a look, a word. Then I touched you and you responded… like you're responding still…."

This zapped her with just enough energy to push out of his arms. "Sure. It's my fault."

He let her put distance between them this time. "There's no fault here. Just the phenomenon that exists between us, this absolute physical affinity we share. But I really didn't intend to kiss you."

"*Kiss* me? That's what you call a kiss?"

A rough huff of self-deprecation escaped him. "So I almost took you standing up, probably would have, not giving a second thought that we're in the middle of your brother's stateroom, if you hadn't stopped me. You have that effect on me. I see you and I can only think of pleasuring you."

Once she'd believed his every word. She'd been certain that what they did share *was* a phenomenon, as undeniable and unstoppable as a force of nature. Then she'd found out the truth. It was clear he thought she didn't know, that he didn't need to invent a new deception.

He approached her again, one of those hands stroking a gossamer touch down her cheek. "But you're wrong. About the last thing you said to me. No matter how many blows to the head I sustain, nothing could make me forget it. You said, *Find yourself someone else who might have a death wish. Because I don't.*"

He remembered. Word for word.

Figured. He was said to possess a computerlike mind, always archiving, networking, extrapolating. On top of his fighting prowess and weapons mastery, it was what made him the ultimate modern warrior and strategist in this information age.

She pulled away from the debilitation of his touch. "And that statement has been solidified by the passage of time and reinforced by this new stunt. So, since you have a flawless memory, what else is wrong with you? Haven't I already turned down your marriage proposal once before?"

Perfect teeth sank into his lip, making her feel they'd sunk into hers again. "I prefer to dwell on when you said yes."

She ignored the tingling of her lips. "Only to follow it with a resounding no, when I came to my senses. Now you're using an impending war to reintroduce the subject? Since it's not faulty memory, I assume these are your new orders?"

Something blipped in his gaze. It was gone before she could fathom it. But even that much from him was telling. He was taken aback and clearly had no idea that she was onto him.

Infusing her tone with all the cool derision she could, she cocked her head at him. "This surprises you? Hmm, maybe I must reconsider all I heard about your reputation as a know-it-all spymaster. Anyway, if you're still not sure what I mean… Yes, I do know. Everything."

Three

She knew. Everything.

For stunned moments that was all that filled Mohab's mind. Then alarm diminished and questions crowded in its place.

What was "everything" according to her? Whatever she thought that was, could that be the reason behind her sudden rejection six years ago?

He stared at her as she stood safe feet away, tall and majestic in a cream skirt suit that made her skin glow, still the most magnificent thing he'd ever seen. Even more than he'd remembered. And he'd thought he remembered everything about this woman whose memory had refused to relinquish its hold over him, whose feel still seethed beneath his skin, whose taste still lingered on his tongue.

But he'd come here today hoping what he remembered had been exaggerated, that his many sightings of her during the past years had perpetuated the delusion, that one up close look would dissipate it.

Then he'd walked into Kamal's stateroom, and one look at her had dashed any hopes he'd ever entertained of finally purging her from his system. Everything he'd remembered about her had been diluted. Or maturity had only intensified her effect on him. He *hadn't* meant to drown in her. But the years of separation, instead of dampening his responses, had only made it impossible for him to ration them.

His gaze swept her ripe curves. His every inch ached, remembering how they'd fit against his angles, how her supple softness had filled his hands, cushioned his hardness, accommodated his demand. His fingers buzzed as they relived skimming her warm, velvet skin, overflowing with her resilient flesh, winding in her silky, raven tresses. His lips and tongue stung with the phantom sensations of feeling hers again, hot and moist and fragrant, surrendering to his invasion, demanding his dominance.

He'd almost taken her, in a near-literal reenactment of their last time together, before saying one word to her. And how she'd responded. He'd felt her every inch vibrate to his frequency, every nerve resonate with his urgency. Even now, after she'd collected herself and retreated behind a barricade of cold contempt, he could still feel it seething. Her mind was another matter, though. If outrage could flay, he'd be minus skin now. He certainly felt as raw as if he was.

So was her rage a reaction to his incursion, or did the developing situation only pile on top of the "everything" she claimed to know?

He could ask, since she seemed to be forthcoming all of a sudden. But he wasn't here to dredge up the past. And if he could still just touch her and they'd both go up in flames, that was all he needed to know.

All he needed, period.

But she was waiting for him to make some kind of response to her revelation. He'd give her one, all right. Just not what she might expect.

He walked back to where she'd retreated. "So you know everything?" At her curt nod, he shoved his hands into his pockets so they wouldn't reach for her again. "Let's test this claim, shall we?"

That twist surprised her. *Zain*. Good. He shouldn't be the only one not knowing if he was coming or going here.

He cocked his head at her. "Do you know that I committed a cardinal sin during that hostage crisis?"

The tangent seemed to confuse her.

When she answered, the modulated voice that had sung its siren song in his ear for years was lower, huskier. "If you mean killing, I know all too well. Those moments, when you stormed the conference hall with your black-ops team and took out our captors, is forever branded in my memory. I watched you…terminate six of our captors single-handedly, with a precision I only thought happened in movies." Those slanting, dense eyebrows he'd loved to trace and lips drew together. "But I didn't think you considered killing a sin. Not in your line of work."

"Killing *is* my line of work. At least, it's part of the job description. Though 'killing' isn't what I call it. I prefer 'eliminating lethal threats to innocents.'"

Her eyes turned a somber cognac as she nodded. She didn't contest that he spoke the simple truth, that people like him were a necessity to control the monsters who roamed the earth. She'd obviously seen enough in *her* line of work to know that his extreme measures were indispensable at times. Just as they had been that day when she'd been taken hostage with five hundred others at that conference in Bidalya.

But she could have contradicted him to score a point. That she didn't, that she remained objective even to the detriment of her own attack, thrilled him.

He sighed. "But the sin I committed had nothing to do with the violence I perpetrated. I committed the cardinal sin of my line of work."

"How so?"

"I deviated from the plan, improvised. I could have gotten so many killed."

Again, counter to his expectations, her eyes grew impassioned as she contradicted him, in *his* defense. "But you saved hundreds, all of us who remained. And you didn't seem to be improvising. You acted with such certainty, such efficiency, it was as if everything had been rehearsed. To the point that it felt as if the captors themselves were playing an exact role in the sequence you designed."

"If it seemed like that to you, it was because of my men's outstanding skills, and because I managed to compensate on the fly. But that doesn't mean I didn't make a huge mistake." Her eyes were puzzled but engrossed. He could tell that she couldn't wait to see where he was taking this. "Do you remember what I did when we stormed in?"

She nodded stiffly, as if it still pained her to think of that harrowing time. And who could blame her? She'd watched three people get killed in cold blood as proof of their captors' resoluteness. She'd once told him that knowing the true meaning of helplessness, failing to protect those people, had damaged her more than her fear of meeting the same fate.

"What do you remember?"

Her exquisite features contorted with the reluctance to conjure up the memories. Still, she answered, "It was so explosive, but I remember it frame for frame. You burst in while one of them was threatening Najeeb that he'd start blowing parts off him. Then I met your eyes across the distance and…and…"

"Go on."

She swallowed. "You streaked toward me, blowing

away those men left and right, and then you were in front of me—shielding me—as you and your team finished off the rest."

"And that was my sin. *Najeeb* was my mission. And I took one look at you across that hall and made the instantaneous decision to save you first."

Her eyes widened; her lips opened on a soundless exclamation. She'd evidently never thought to question what he'd done.

When she finally talked, her whisper was impeded. "But you blasted away the one who was threatening him as you ran to me. You gave no one a chance to use him as shield or to harm him."

"I should have run *to* him, should have shielded *him*. As my crown prince, he should have been my only priority. Instead, I made that you."

"But you managed to save him and everyone else."

"Only because I managed to compensate, as I said. Najeeb could have gotten shot before I ended the threat to him. And knowing full well the widespread damage his injury or death would have caused, retaliations that would have reaped far more than five hundred lives, I still risked that."

Time seemed to stretch as bewilderment glimmered in her gemlike eyes.

She let out a shaky breath. "So what are you saying? That you took one look at me and were so bowled over you decided to risk everyone's lives—including your own—for *me?*"

"No. That's not what I'm saying. I was…bowled over a bit before that."

He watched her mouth drop open. This was news to her. He'd never intimated that he'd seen her before that day. But he'd seen her over two years earlier, had searched her out many times afterward.

"But it was the first time I'd seen you!"

"I saw no upside in letting you see me, or in acting on my interest. You were, as you pointed out so many times when we were together, an Aal Masood…and I was an Aal Ghaanem. The Montagues and Capulets didn't have a thing on our moronically feuding houses. I also didn't think it would be wise or fair to ever involve a woman in my crazy existence." He exhaled. "Then I saw you in danger and every rational thought flew out the window."

Her eyes filled with so much; he struggled not to drag her to him and kiss them closed.

Then they emptied of everything, leaving only hardness. "Why are you telling me this now?"

He shrugged. "I am testing your claim that you know everything. I just proved that you don't."

"You proved only that you spin a good yarn. As I already knew you did. Is this one supposed to appeal to my ego?"

A mirthless huff escaped him. "You think I'm making this up? Why? To butter you up for my current purposes? I wish. As someone who knows what a bullet feels like ripping through my flesh, I would have preferred one to admitting how fallible I am, how unprofessional I was, how I risked everyone's lives to protect a woman who didn't know me…whom I believed could never be mine."

Steel mixed with gold in her gaze, clearly not buying his admissions. Funny. If he'd ever thought he'd confess this to her, he wouldn't have dreamed this would be her reaction.

Might as well confess the rest, let her make whatever she wished of it. "When I burst in and I met your eyes, saw that mixture of terror and courage and fury…I couldn't imagine I wouldn't be able to look in those eyes again, to get the chance to know you. My instincts took over…and I let them."

She averted those eyes, depriving him of their touch.

"Yet after you went to such lengths to save me, you didn't follow up on your wish to 'know' me. Not for over a year."

He exhaled heavily. "I might have saved the day, for you and for everyone else, but *I* knew how badly I messed up. I guess I was punishing myself for failing to fulfill my duty and couldn't reward my failure by giving myself the gift of knowing you, the one behind my lapse."

She raised her eyes, that derision back in full force. "So was it guilt that stopped you from giving yourself the 'gift' of knowing me, or was it that you didn't think it 'wise or fair' to involve a woman in your crazy existence?"

"Both. And the family feud. Everything."

"Then, a year later, you just decided to disregard all those overpowering reasons you had not to approach me. Once you made that first contact, you relentlessly courted me all the way to your bed. Then, before I could catch my breath, you pushed for marriage. And when I tried to slow things down, you pushed harder. And when I decided to put a stop to it, you threatened you'd slander me and destroy any man who came near me."

He gritted his teeth on the memory of his despair, when he'd felt her slipping through his fingers. "These were my most indefensible moments. Trying to hang on to you, then going almost berserk when I couldn't."

"Yeah, sure," she scoffed. "You lost control out of sheer emotion. That coming from the ice-cold man they sent after the Mata Haris of the world, to seduce, entrap and destroy them."

It was his turn to blink in surprise. She knew that? How?

She elaborated on just how much she knew. "I've been told how you are the man to rely on when a woman is involved, the incomparable undercover agent no female can resist. You're not only known as *Al Moddammer,* but *Qatel an-Nesaa*—the lady-killer. And you're claiming you took one look at the twenty-year-old nobody I was, an obscure member of your family's hereditary enemies, and couldn't think straight on account of my irresistibility?"

He exhaled. "That does about sum it up."

"Tut."

That click of her tongue shot straight to his loins. Any second now he was going to ravish her again, come what may.

Unaware of his state, she went on, "I expected better from the ultimate secret-service weapon that you are. Some airtight premise, at least something more plausible. Seems I have to revise many things I believed about you. You do remember I prefaced this unfortunate encounter, before you took that detour into badly scripted drama, by mentioning that I know everything, don't you?"

"Again I say I wish it was anything but the pathetic truth. So, against all my intentions, I find myself forced to ask, according to you, what *is* everything?"

Her eyes became icy embers. "Everything from the moment I went to meet Najeeb and found you waiting for me instead."

Jala watched those eyes of his blaze at her declaration.

She'd never been able to decide when they were most hypnotic: when they glowed with a constant flame or when they fluctuated—as they'd been doing throughout this confrontation—their pupils expanding and constricting, giving the intense tawny irises the illusion of burning coals.

She'd dreamed of those fiery eyes, his voice, his touch, for over a year after the hostage crisis. And it had had nothing to do with his saving her life. He'd just…overwhelmed her. He'd melted her just by looking at her, just by being near. When feeling that way had been totally out of character for her. She'd been too mature for her age, as her brothers had always told her. Cerebral, almost jaded.

But Mohab…he *had* bowled her over. For over a year, she'd relived every single second of being pressed against the body he'd fearlessly offered as her shield. She'd suffocated with remembered terror that a bullet could tear through his perfection. Then she'd relived every second as he'd sheltered her away from the scene of carnage. But before she could have even a word with him, the Bidalyan government had bundled all the hostages, sending them back to their countries to close that case as quickly as possible.

For months afterward, she'd gone crazy trying to find out who he was. Until Najeeb, her fellow hostage, had sought her out.

Najeeb had been magnificent during the crisis. Level-headed, fearless, shrewd, he'd managed their captors like a veteran used to being under fire. It was certain more people would have died if not for his intervention. He'd recognized her as the only one he could depend on and they'd forged an instantaneous bond, as if they'd always worked together, minimizing damages for two agonizing days.

Then one of their captors had cracked, started shrieking he'd blow bits off Najeeb, as the highest-ranking royal, so his father would pressure the Bidalyans to meet their demands faster. But just as the situation had escalated, Mohab had exploded onto the scene.

It had surprised her to find out from Najeeb that their savior had been the head of Saraya's special forces, not Bidalya's. Turned out Bidalya had ceded control of the hostage retrieval to Mohab so he'd be responsible for his crown prince's fate, and because he was the best at what he did.

But finding out he was also Najeeb's older paternal cousin had dashed even her fantasies. Najeeb could be her friend in spite of their families' enmity. But friendship wasn't what she'd wanted from Mohab. Not that she'd thought she'd see him again.

Then, one day, he'd just appeared, instead of Najeeb, to escort her to her first award ceremony. She'd been so delirious with this windfall she hadn't questioned how or why. Even when Najeeb had called, explaining the emergency that would keep him away for months and hadn't mentioned sending Mohab, she hadn't thought it odd. She'd taken everything Mohab had said as uncontestable truth.

That first evening had been magical, and he'd been the perfect companion. He'd suggested lunch the next day and she'd jumped at his invitation, had continued to grab every opportunity to be with him for the next two months, with Mohab showing her more facets of himself, each impossible to resist.

Not that resisting had been a consideration. Then, as if he'd known just when she'd become ready for more, he'd taken her to his penthouse, and then he'd taken her....

"Will you answer my question, or will you keep the 'everything' you know a mystery?"

His taunt pulled her out of the plunge into the past, which appeared to have been only a moment in real time.

She was loath to dredge up the sordid past, but she'd cornered herself into doing just that.

What the hell.

She leveled her best denigrating gaze on him. "How is it a mystery when we both know you only entered my life to eliminate me from Najeeb's? That I was just another mission to *Qatel an-Nesaa?*"

Four

Jala watched his pupils expand until it looked as if his eyes were being engulfed by black holes.

He finally inhaled. "What's the source of your info?"

"What do you think?"

"Najeeb." It was a statement. "What did he tell you?"

"The truth."

A long exhalation, then Mohab moved, brushing past her on his way to the couch. He sat down in one of those movements of pure power and grace. "I injured my knee in my last mission, so standing isn't a favorite activity at the moment." When she only stared down at him, he sighed. "I also pulled a muscle in my neck."

His perfectly formed hand caressed the space beside him, enticing her to fill it, making her feel it over her back, below her panties, kneading and owning all over again.

She gritted her teeth against the resurgence of lust. "And I should care about your discomfort? The man who's responsible for dragging me back to this godforsaken region and behind this farce that's causing me nothing but discomfort?"

"Point taken. But this will take longer than I expected and it would alleviate at least your physical discomfort if you sit for the duration."

"Actually, this won't take *any* longer. I already told you to go to hell. I'm sure you chest-thumping males will find another way to settle your war once you give up on me as a convenient chess piece in your backward power games."

She thought she was safely out of his range, but when she turned away it was her hand he snagged this time. Her balance was so compromised she needed only a coaxing tug to tumble over him.

Breath burst from her lungs as her body impacted his, even when it did so softly. His effortless power supported most of her weight in midplummet, arranging her to land across his body, one arm cushioning her back, the other gathering her thighs over his lap.

Before she could even recoil, he flattened her breasts to the expanse of his chest, swamping her in the intoxication of his scent and heat. "I'm a breath away from picking up where we left off, Jala. This time, neither of us will be able to stop. So if you don't want me to make love to you right here on your brother's couch, distract me."

She hated him, but herself more, for knowing he'd only spoken the truth. All her pleasure centers were revving, her body readying itself for him. Craving *had* been seething beneath her skin all this time. She had to end this before he exploited that weakness. More than he already had.

"Would a poke in the eye be distracting enough for you? Or do you prefer something bitten off?"

"I'd take any voluntary touch from you, but—" he released her thighs and scooped her hands into his palms "—I'd prefer not to add to my injuries right now. There's another thing that would dampen my arousal. Having this out at last. Talk to me."

"I already said all I had to say, then and now."

"All right. I'll do the talking. So Najeeb told you 'the truth.'" She nodded, hoping to lull him enough so she'd be able to squirm away with as little indignity as possible. He sighed, pressing his chest harder into her. "Truths are over-rated, points of view and perspectives at best. So tell me his version, what you sanctioned as the only one there is."

"I'll play your aggravating game on one condition."

"Let you go?" Her glare said that didn't deserve the oxygen it would take to say yes. He sighed deeper. "I doubt anything you say can be worth not holding you like this."

A growl rolled in her gut. "I would have preferred to end this with your dignity and appendages intact, but at this point, I'm not against screaming bloody murder to get rid of you. The royal guard won't care who you are. By the time I pull them off you, you'll have more than a creaking knee and neck."

The smile playing across his cruelly sensuous lips became a full-fledged grin, as if she'd just made him a delightful promise. "I had this discussion with your brother a few days ago, about who'd win in such a confrontation—his royal guard or me with my hands tied behind my back."

And the worst part? She could believe the odds *would* be in his favor. Damn him.

"But since I can't risk your brother's current goodwill if I damage his soldiers, I'll pass on a demonstration."

He released her, oh, so slowly, and she felt nerves spooling inside every inch that separated from him. Even withdrawing his touch was as exquisite as bestowing it.

Ya Ullah...why was she so afflicted? Why was he the only man who'd ever accessed her controls and so... uncontrollably? How was her mental and emotional aversion so divorced from her sensual response? Why was it so absolute?

And he knew exactly what he was doing to her; he was playing her responses like a virtuoso. A ruthless expert in manipulating the female body and psyche.

Najeeb had told her Mohab had played many women before her. As, no doubt, he had countless others after her. Probably during. Not ones like the inexperienced and already infatuated young woman she'd been, but cunning, jaded women who'd seen and done it all, even hardened criminals and spies. Yet he'd still taken them in with his overwhelming sexuality and perfectly simulated charm and chivalry. She hadn't had a chance.

A new wave of mortification poured strength into her limbs as she pushed away from him. He didn't help her this time, forcing her to dip with all her weight into his unyielding power for support. The way he threw his head back against the back of the couch, his rumble of enjoyment as her fingers sank into his muscles, the way his heavy lids lowered, turning his eyes to burning slits as he watched her struggle up, assailed her with the memory of all the times he'd looked and sounded like that as she'd ridden him to oblivion....

Severing contact, she thought she'd managed to escape his compulsion when he ensnared her again.

Holding her head in the cradle of his hands, striking her immobile with his very gentleness, he exhaled softly. "Just one more."

Then he took her lips in a kiss that all but extracted her soul.

She took it all, helpless to do anything but let him invade her with pleasure, her body singing in delight, weeping with need. After a series of conquering plunges, he slowed to clinging plucks that had her almost keeling over him again. He finally relinquished her lips with a last groan of regret.

Feeling her legs had turned to jelly, she barely reached the facing armchair before collapsing on it.

"I hope you've had your fun."

At her rasp, his eyes simmered like some supernatural beast's. "You know I didn't. You know exactly how I have fun. Hard, protracted, borderline-fatal-with-pleasure fun."

She managed not to shudder. Yeah. She knew. Every cell in her body seemed to know nothing else. They'd had mega doses of "fun" in the five months they'd been intimate. Whenever she'd thought it couldn't get better, it had, like a force picking up momentum. Familiarity had only kept shifting the addiction to higher gears. It had been so intense, had felt so pure, it had been a devastating blow when she'd learned the truth.

Exhaling the remembered misery, she made her decision. Letting your enemy find out how much you knew wasn't wise, but maybe getting it all out would help purge it—and him—from her system once and for all.

"Let's start with when Najeeb left New York. Or shall we say when you set up the emergencies he'd been called back to Saraya to handle, with his father allegedly sick and unable to deal with them."

His eyes lost that languid sensuality, but there was no other sign of response.

She went on. "For months everything seemed to thwart him, and he grew suspicious, decided to go to the source of all info—his mother. After making him swear he'd never confront his father, Queen Safaa admitted that King Hassan believed Najeeb would end up marrying me, a daughter of the hated Aal Masoods, and it would cost him his position as his heir, as Saraya's tribes wouldn't abide the introduction of Aal Masood blood into the royal family.

He even feared the Aal Ghaanems might lose the throne altogether to an uprising."

Mohab still had no reaction. But then again, why should he react? He already knew all this.

She exhaled. "To stop this calamity, King Hassan had one hope of breaking up our relationship. You. The kingdom's most lethal secret weapon. I was a homeland security threat of the highest order after all. As someone who was raised to despise the Aal Masoods, the idea that your crown prince might sully your line with the blood of your hated enemies was probably as unthinkable to you.

"Najeeb's mother related how you shared your king's opinion of me—the then-minor princess who flaunted her region's values and disgraced her brothers by living a degenerate life in the West. You agreed that I was manipulating the honorable Najeeb, using our shared ordeal to ride him to the status of a future queen. When the king authorized you to get rid of me, he knew how you'd do it. The same way you rid the kingdom of every black widow who tried to compromise the royal family or the integrity of the kingdom."

His gaze remained unchanged, betraying nothing.

Figured. He'd betrayed nothing through their five-month relationship. Not one action or glance or word had given her a clue that it had all been an act. The reverse had been true. Everything from him had been fierce, consistent, unequivocal, had felt more real than anything she'd ever experienced. Discovering the truth had hit so out of the blue, it had crushed her.

Her world had warped, every emotion and passion she'd felt for him becoming shame, humiliation.

She went on, emptying her voice of any remembered anguish. "You seduced me only to make me ineligible for Najeeb, then asked me to marry you to perfect your act, no doubt to drop me like a used napkin the moment you were sure your crown prince was safe."

Najeeb had been livid at his father, but more at Mohab, if only for the interference, the duplicity. His outrage had been mitigated by his belief that he'd saved her in time. She had never exposed the depths of her fall and folly to her friend. Only wanting the mess over with, she'd made Najeeb promise he'd never confront Mohab. She'd just wanted to walk away.

Numb and feeling used, she'd stumbled home, had stood in that shower for what might have been hours. Then Mohab had come. His urgency and passion, which her senses still hadn't been able to recognize as fake, had had her body detonating with a fireball of lust and her mind spiraling in blankness.

Afterward everything had spilled over, razing her with the devastation of fury and mortification.

After Mohab had finally gone, she'd collapsed. Not in any dramatic way, just a gradual descent into depression, her misery deepening with time and repercussions. It had taken her years to climb out.

Now, just as she was finally over her ordeal and firmly on stable footing, the man responsible for it all had come back to destroy the peace she'd struggled so long and hard for.

"So that's why you decided you didn't want to marry me after all, and so abruptly."

His deep statement roused her from her musings.

She gave him the only answer he'd get from her. "It just gave me the reason to bail, as I'd been wanting to, without caring how I did it."

"That's why you didn't confront me, no matter how much I pushed? You weren't interested in hearing my defense, since you'd already decided to walk out on me?"

At her nod, he shook his head, as if deprecating himself for wanting to hear her discoveries *had* been the only reason behind her rejection. No doubt out of pride, as that would make her the only woman who had walked away from him. Buying her claim didn't make things better, but it *was* something, since she'd rather crawl back to the airport in today's heat wave rather than give him the triumph of knowing how fully he'd taken her in.

"So craving me was one thing, marrying me was another."

"Who said I craved you?"

His mock reproving look sent blood surging to her loins. "Let's not dispute the indisputable, *ya jameelati*. You did, and I just proved you still do."

Her insides clenched at his taunt, his calling her his beauty. "I'm just a hot-blooded woman."

"That's why you were a virgin when I first took you?"

The way he said *took you* reverberated in her being.

For there was no other way to describe what he'd done to her that first night. Or any other time after that. He'd shown her what her body and being had always been capable of, but would have lain untapped if not for his unlocking their potential. Her wildest dreams before him hadn't known to venture into the realms where he'd taken her.

But she'd still woken up in his arms that first time feeling anxious. Though she'd believed him to be progressive, Saraya was even more ultraconservative than Judar, and she'd feared he might despise her for surrendering to him outside the marriage bed. She feared that because it would have meant he wasn't the man she'd fallen in love with. And if he did, she would have considered him worth nothing but good riddance, but it would still have wounded her terribly.

But he'd assuaged her fears as soon as he'd opened his eyes. He'd seamlessly played his part, had been euphoric, indulgent, even poetic about how proud he'd been that she'd bestowed her innocence on him, given him the honor of initiating her into intimacy. Then he'd asked her to marry him.

Even though she'd never thought of marriage, except to reject it, she'd found herself saying yes....

"Well?"

His challenge reminded her she hadn't answered his taunt. "Oh, you're harping on my being a virgin at the advanced age of twenty-one? A young woman still struggling to leave her stiflingly conservative upbringing behind? You expected me to go to the States and hop into bed with every man I fancied?"

"You'd been there for three years. Enough time to change your outlook and behavior, especially at that age, if you'd wanted to. But you fancied no one. I was your first. In every way. I know."

"You mean as the infallible intelligence god you are?"

"No. As the man who awakened you."

Damn him. He saw too much, knew everything.

"And once I *awakened,* thanks to your expert... rousing..."

"Nothing happened. You didn't replace me in your bed."

She gaped at him. How did he...? Did that mean...?

Before she could blow a valve, he went on calmly, "*This* I know as the incomparable intelligence god that I am."

If people could explode, Jala would have, Mohab thought.

He'd tripped the one wire that could set her off. One of *two* wires. The first was passion, which he was gratified he could still trigger with a touch. The second was privacy.

It had always been her biggest hang-up. She'd been near obsessive about it. Her insistence on never meeting him where anyone might recognize her had at first made him think it was a cunning effort to have his cake and eat Najeeb's, too. But as his preconceptions had melted, and she'd opened up with details of her life in Judar, he'd understood how hard-won her autonomy had been. After a lifetime of having her breaths counted and steps monitored, she'd sworn...*no more*.

He watched her rise, every inch aching to have her in his arms again. But that wouldn't move anything forward. And he was afraid that if she surrendered again, he wouldn't be able to stop.

"You had me under surveillance?" she seethed.

He sighed. Not his favorite topic, discussing his obsession with her. "I'm not good at letting go."

"Sure. Do you have a bridge to sell me with that? So what was it, really? You forgot to call off my surveillance detail and reports kept hitting your desk?"

At his raised eyebrow, she took a furious step toward him. "We're in full-disclosure mode, aren't we? So how about you not pretend you didn't have my every move documented before you approached me? It's evident you formulated a plan to entrap me in the most time-efficient manner based on my character analysis. But after you ended my supposed threat to your crown prince, what purpose did keeping tabs on me serve? Was it to make sure I didn't go after another of your kingdom's princes after you made sure Najeeb found me 'ineligible' to be his future queen?"

Wincing at the words that had haunted him with shame, he shook his head. "I didn't tell Najeeb anything."

"I don't believe you."

Her instantaneous rejection was what he deserved. Not only had he threatened to do just that, Najeeb *had* cut off all relations with her, proving to her that Mohab had carried out his threat.

But he hadn't. He'd lived dreading news of her impending marriage to Najeeb. When that had never come to pass, he'd found out why. His uncle had told Najeeb that Mohab *had* fulfilled his mission in proving that Jala was dissolute, but if Najeeb desired her, he could enjoy her, as Mohab once had.

Even though he'd been hurt and jealous, believed she'd chosen Najeeb over him, he'd also come to admit that she'd had every right to change her mind about marrying him. And he'd been *furious* that Najeeb had ended what he'd professed to be a strong friendship based on hearsay, or even the truth of their relationship. If that made her dissolute in Najeeb's eyes, when the man hadn't staked a prior claim, it made him despicable.

He'd been unable to abide his uncle's defamation and his cousin's desertion of her. In a gesture of ultimate contempt, he'd resigned his job and left their and Saraya's service.

He exhaled. "Ask Najeeb. He'll tell you I haven't talked to him since that night. You had every right to leave me, and I'll be forever ashamed I threatened to slander you for it."

Her glare wavered only to harden again. "Even if I believe that, you have other transgressions waiting in line. How dare you have me followed?"

Savoring the bewitching sight she made in her fury, he said, "As long as I'm already damned, and I have no hope of having the extenuating circumstances sanctioned, I might as well tell you that I've been keeping tabs on you far longer than you think. I started right after I first saw you attending a conference with your oldest brother Farooq in Washington."

Her eyes rounded. "That was ten years ago!"

"*Aih.* You were only eighteen and the most incredible thing I'd ever seen. I felt the chemistry that sizzles between us singe me even then, even when you didn't see me."

Her disbelief was almost palpable. "It's not *possible* I didn't see you."

"You do remember what I do for a living, don't you? If I want to stay out of sight, that's where I remain."

But he'd been unable to stop following her after that first sighting. He'd known he'd never approach her, but she'd become his fantasy when he'd never had one before.

Then that hostage crisis had happened. Her name had been the only thing he'd seen on that hostage list before he'd stormed in, and he'd made the decision to save her first right then. Facing that had made him more enraged at himself, his anger mounting the more he found himself struggling not to go after her, and to hell with all the reasons to stay away.

"And you expect me to believe you were enthralled at first sight? A sight I didn't even reciprocate?"

"Seems you never looked in the mirror."

"C'mon…you have tons of gorgeous women littering your path, and I'm not even that. I'm too…androgynous."

An incredulous laugh burst out of him. "Then I don't know what that says about me, since you define femininity to me." Before she ricocheted with another rebuttal, he cut her off. "Aren't you going to hear my version of what happened?"

"Will you tell me Najeeb or I jumped to conclusions, or some other lameness like that? Don't bother. I already told you I don't care. It was just a welcome bit of news that made breaking up with you much easier."

He had to accept that. It seemed he hadn't realized how controlling his kind of life had made him, how severely allergic she had been, and still was, to any infringement on her free will. Her distress *had* been acute every time he'd pushed to announce their engagement. She'd kept saying she wanted more private time before their families and their feud infringed on their relationship. It seemed the more he tried to push for moving forward, the more she'd resented his attempts to herd her toward his objective. She would probably have ended it on that account alone. Her discoveries about his subterfuge had just rushed everything to its conclusion.

He patted the space beside him again. "You still need to know my side, just so you know 'everything' for real."

She only flung a dismissing hand at him. "Suit yourself."

"Thank you, Your Ungraciousness." He bowed his head mockingly. "So…when my uncle assigned me the mission of sabotaging you and Najeeb, I pounced on it, but only as a pretext to finally approaching you. That alone made me wonder if you might be as dangerous as my uncle believed. After all, how could you be the sweet innocent I thought you to be if you affected *me* this way, when the world's most lethal seductresses didn't turn a hair in me? If I was so enthralled from afar, what chance did Najeeb have?"

He *had* approached her, hoping she'd turn out to be nothing like his fantasies and he could end her hold over him. Saving Najeeb would have been incidental.

But from that first night, he'd lost sight of the whole world in her company, then of his own reality in her arms. He'd forgotten who he was and what kind of life he led to the point he'd asked her to marry him.

"But you changed your mind once you were with me, right?"

"When I was with you I *had* no mind. But if anyone gets your reservations back then, it's me. You had your reasons for shunning marriage, and I had mine."

Not that his dread had stopped him from wanting to go through with it, from becoming progressively more impatient with her postponements, even when he hadn't realized they'd been signs of trouble. This obliviousness had been why he'd been so shocked when she'd ended it. Then, after he'd found out why she hadn't hooked up with Najeeb, she'd disappeared.

He'd turned the world upside down searching for her, to no avail. He'd only found her when she'd resurfaced on her own, following a yearlong humanitarian trek in uncharted areas in South America. He hadn't let her out of his sight since.

And all the while, he'd been seeking a pretext to go after her again. Now that he'd finally found it, he would get her. She just didn't know it yet.

He swept her in an aching glance. "But my proposal, as ill-advised as it was, *was* real." At her disbelieving huff, his lips twisted. "Whatever you think I thought or felt, not even I can feign that much hunger, for that long or at all."

"But men don't have to feign anything. Put a willing woman in their bed and that's all she wrote."

"Your inexperience with anyone else but me is showing." He rose, savoring every nuance of her chagrin at being unable to contest his exclusive ownership of her body. "Those indiscriminate men you describe are aroused by the novelty, the challenge. They are notorious for losing…steam quickly when with a familiar body, no matter how tempting. But the more I had you, the more my hunger for you raged. I craved you enough that I would have jumped into an inferno—or even into marriage—to keep you."

"Then it's fortunate Najeeb's revelations pushed me to make the decision I'd been circling for a while, saving us both from a fate worse than hell."

"I'm just telling you my side. And now that you've told me yours, I understand why you walked away. A combination of commitment phobia, resentment and outrage is pretty potent. You were doing what you believed was right for yourself. But that's your mind. What about your body? How long did it ache in demand for mine? How severe were the withdrawal pangs?"

Something dark and enormous expanded in her eyes.

His heart hammered. *Ya Ullah,* was that…anguish?

The disturbing expression was gone before he could be sure he'd seen it. "I can tell you for a fact that for the next year there was no aching or withdrawal."

That didn't sound like a spiteful denial. She meant this.

Could it be she'd walked away at no cost to herself? There'd been no emptiness in her gut and loins, no burning in her senses and skin, needing his assuagement, his completion? Could the love she'd sobbed out loud in pleasure-drenched nights have evaporated so absolutely that not even a remnant of the physical yearning remained?

No. He wouldn't buy that. She'd melted again at his touch. Her body still proclaimed him its mate and master.

As if to contradict his conviction, she said, "I haven't had other men since because I was too busy with work, and I'm not the kind for one-night stands. It wasn't because I was pining for you."

"If you'd found the intensity of attraction and totality of arousal you had with me, you would have made time. But you wanted that or nothing at all. Sometimes hunger is so vast, nothing but what you crave would fulfill it." Giving her no chance to back away, he took her in his arms. "I know, because nothing could fulfill my craving but you."

"Yeah, sure." She squirmed, only inflaming him more.

He hauled her tighter against him. "Fact is sometimes stranger than fiction. It was as unreal to me as it sounds to you now. This chemistry we share wasn't only an aphrodisiac, but a mind-altering substance."

"Sounds like something you wouldn't want to abuse. So why are you doing this? Or are you just making the best of your 'mission' this time, too?"

"This time, it's all me. How much has Kamal told you?"

Sullenly, she told him. Kamal had only told her the general situation, hadn't even mentioned him by name. So he now filled in his part of the story, leaving out only that he could abort the hostilities without her marrying him.

She digested everything, inert in his arms, eyes somber. "So you're going to be king. That's unexpected. But it also enables you to resolve this without little Aal Masood me."

Her analytical powers were unerring. As he well knew.

But he couldn't corroborate her analysis or this was over before it began. "The peace through marriage is what my uncle would agree to."

"How ironic. I was the only woman he couldn't abide for his heir, now I'm the only one to serve his purposes." She pushed away, hard. "He can go to hell, right along with you."

He hated to play this card, but he'd run out of options. "You once said you would repay me one day."

That made her go rock still, a world of reproach filling her cognac eyes. "I also said I won't do that with my life."

"I'm not asking for your life. Just your hand in marriage. Just your body in my bed."

A scoff burst from her. "My choice, my future and my body. That just about wraps up what makes up my life."

He shrugged. "Not really."

"Oh? What else is there that you're not laying claim to?"

"Plenty. Your heart, your mind, your soul." At her immovable glare, he found no recourse but to push. "I *am* collecting my debt now, Jala. It is that imperative." For him.

Apprehension gradually replaced ire on her exquisite face.

Then she finally exclaimed, "You're all really going to do something insane if we don't get married?"

And he seized that first wavering in her resolve, drove his advantage home. "We have to get married. Nobody said we have to *stay* married."

Five

Jala couldn't believe it.

That gargantuan weasel had made her say yes.

He'd used his every weapon, from seduction to logic to cajoling, playing havoc with her vulnerabilities and convictions, making her revoke her edict consigning him to hell.

But then, the situation *was* dire.

From her work in regions festering with conflict, she was too familiar with how wars ignited over much less than the current stakes. In places like their region, where pride and tribalism and other inherited, obsolete conventions still ruled to a great degree beneath the modernized veneer, once blood was spilled, enmities could—and did—rage for centuries.

Kamal and Mohab, damn them both to hell, had pegged her accurately. They'd both counted on her inability to stand by and let something like this happen if she could help it. They'd known that after her first shock and outrage, once she realized it was true only she could help, she would.

But she drew the line at marrying Mohab to do it. The best she'd do was agree to a fake engagement.

Yeah, another one. But one she *knew* was fake. She'd go through the motions for the sake of peace.

And that was *huge* of her. Engagements around here were excruciating, rife with maddening customs and obscene intrusions. Wedding preparations made some of the war zones she'd been to look peaceful.

But she'd use those torturous rituals to draw out this charade until treaties were signed. Then she'd bail out.

One thing still had her red-alert sensors clanging, though. The ease with which Mohab had agreed to her terms.

At first, he'd insisted only an actual marriage would appease King Hassan, that they'd have to dispense with an engagement to give him the quick union that would force him from his warpath. He'd suggested a six-month period before separating. According to him, that was enough time to settle all treaties and resolve all disputes.

But when she'd countered with the most she'd agree to, and that he'd have to convince King Hassan to sign the treaties *during* their pseudoengagement, he'd consented with disturbing equanimity.

Suddenly she felt as though a rocket had gone off inside her head. She knew *why* his acquiescence had disturbed her. Because it must have been what that insidious rat had been after all the time!

He must have anticipated her first point-blank refusal. So he'd let her get this out of her system. Being ruthlessly results oriented, he must have known an agreement wouldn't be a possibility. The best he could expect from this first encounter was to stall her, stop her from leaving Judar and secure any level of cooperation.

So he'd kept applying pressure here so she'd sidestep there, pushed and pulled, kissed and caressed, laid bare secrets, exhumed heartaches, appealed to her ego and seared her senses in a steady barrage. When he'd felt her waver, he'd hit her with a solution that had too high a cost. At this point, he must have projected two outcomes. Since she'd already entered the cooperative zone, either she'd buckle and accept outright, or she'd counter with her own offer, bargaining a lower price. Either way, he'd achieve his objective. Her, here, playing along.

That it was only for now and not for real didn't bother him. This was only round one to him. Being Machiavellian and a long-term thinker, he most certainly wouldn't abide by the limits of what she'd granted. And as a master strategist, he had every reason to expect he wouldn't have to. If he'd gotten her to concede that much in under two hours, he'd probably estimated he'd have her dancing to his tune in two days.

She was now certain he would keep on giving her as much rope as she asked for…and use it to lasso and truss her up.

Consternation bubbled on a stifled shriek. She even stomped her foot. It landed with a damp thud on the sand, not the satisfying bang she'd needed.

Groaning in frustration, her gaze jerked around the four-mile shore. Still alone. At least, apparently so.

But of course she wasn't alone. Kamal must have given his guards orders to keep out of her sight. He wouldn't want to infringe on her personal space, aggravating her more than he'd already had.

But there was no doubt dozens of eyes were watching *the* princess of Judar taking a stroll along the shore surrounding the royal palace. She wondered why they'd even bother. No one came within ten miles of the palace or its extensive grounds, by land or by sea. It wasn't even one of those days when the palace and satellite buildings were open for tourists. The only way someone could target her would be by satellite or long-range missile.

Oh, well. She had known what kind of intrusions she'd signed on for the moment she'd agreed to stay in Judar and play Mohab's game. The kind that had once had her running to the States and hiding in blessed anonymity and heavenly aloneness.

The first eighteen years of her life here had surely taken their toll. Though she loved her brothers fiercely, her experience in Judar had been the opposite of theirs in every respect. Even if, at the time, they'd just been three of the former king's multitude of nephews, they'd been everything the region and the royal family valued. Male, magnificent, with personal assets running out of their ears. They'd had every freedom, along with privilege and power, to counter all the responsibilities, expectations and pressures.

While she, the unplanned child her parents had had twelve years after they thought they were done having children, had been a mistake—and a female one at that. To compound her problems, when she'd been only three her mother had been diagnosed with cancer. After a long struggle, when she'd been forced to relinquish Jala's upbringing to others, she'd died when Jala was ten. Less than a year later, her father, totally destroyed by his wife's long illness and death, had died, too, leaving Jala to the care of her older brothers, relatives and hired help.

The next years had been a nightmare. Her brothers, while they'd doted on her, had been too busy forging their success to have much time for her. As one who hated to ask for help or attention, she'd never let them know of her dismal state of mind. She'd felt isolated from the royal family, and from her culture, where she'd never felt she fit in.

But as she'd grown older, she'd been progressively more besieged by the restrictions that being female in Judar entailed, compounded by the fact that she had no mother to fend for her. And while she had enough royal status to suffer its downsides, she had enjoyed none of its advantages. Her situation had been further complicated when she'd refused the privileges offered women here, which she considered condescending and sexist, making her an outcast among her peers. By the time she was finished high school, she'd felt she'd do something drastic if she didn't get away.

Then her maternal aunt's husband was appointed the ambassador of Judar to the United States. Frantic to make use of this possible ticket out, she'd hounded her brothers until they'd agreed to let her go with their aunt to continue her education there. She'd arrived in the States four months before her eighteenth birthday and had left her aunt's custody the day after her birthday party.

Seizing on her freedom of choice at once, she'd started fulfilling her lifelong ambition to follow Farooq in his humanitarian relief efforts.

It had been while attending that ill-fated conference in Bidalya that she'd first set eyes on Mohab. And it had been during the ceremony where she'd received her first work-related award that he'd effectively entered her life.

Now he'd reentered it. And she was back in Judar.

And it was all because of him.

Mohab. Even his name aggravated her right now. His parents had to give him such a lofty one, didn't they? And he had to be an exasperating bastard and live up to it, didn't he? Awe-inspiring. Feared. Even frightening. And he'd gone on to be far more. Spellbinding. Overwhelming. Devastating.

Okay. It wasn't all because of him. This impending war wasn't of his orchestration. And the cruel twist of fate that made her the king of Judar's sister, and Mohab the imminent king of Jareer, was also beyond him.

But now she thought of it, another thing was his fault. Their whole confrontation last evening.

After that preemptive opening seduction scene, he'd proceeded to scramble her entrenched belief that she'd just been another body and mission to him, asserting that he'd wanted her for far longer than she'd even thought. He'd claimed he'd monitored her for years, compromised his duty and disregarded his orders for her, craved her so much that he'd proposed for real. And all along, he'd kept pulling her back into mindlessness, as if he'd been unable to keep his passion in check.

Then she'd agreed to play her part and he'd just… stopped. He'd stood by calmly and just let her leave.

Did that mean everything he'd told her had been more manipulation designed to shove her into the slot where he needed her? Then, once he had, he'd just retracted his tentacles and settled back into neutral mode?

That made the most sense. She *had* long ago become reconciled to the fact that a man who'd chosen Mohab's line of work must be made of a different material than other human beings. To deal with the atrocities he was required to face head-on, he must have long since shut down his basic human emotions. And to fulfill his stealth missions, he must have become an expert at simulating those emotions at will.

But even knowing that, he'd managed to fool her again. He'd anesthetized her judgment and nullified her instincts. She'd actually begun believing his claims and had all but drowned in his passion. His nonexistent passion.

And that was the worst of it all. That after everything that had happened, her senses and responses would forever remain dependent on a mirage. Like Tantalus, she was destined to shrivel up with thirst for an illusion.

What kind of fate was it that always made her his target, his chess piece? Why had fate infected her with this unremitting hunger that nothing had ever eradicated, when he felt none for her, for real, in return? Why, after she'd suppressed it for years until she'd thought she'd been cured, had it taken only his reappearance to drag it out of her depths? And now that the fever had spiked again, how could she subdue it, at least enough to keep on functioning?

A wave of too-familiar dejection crashed over her as she slit her eyes against the brilliant setting sun, suddenly cold to her marrow in the balmy March breeze.

Legs heavy and numb, she started back to the palace. And, in spite of everything, it took her breath all over again.

Anyone looking at it would think it was a historical monument, but she'd attended its inauguration as the new seat of power in Judar just eleven years ago during her late uncle's rule. It had since become a monument as important as the Taj Mahal, and sure gave that legendary edifice a run for its money. It was still as mind-boggling to her as it had been the first time she'd seen it.

Nestled in an extensively landscaped park and surrounded by silver beaches and emerald waters, it crouched in the middle of the peninsula, its grounds almost covered like a massive starship from beyond the stars. Now in the golden drape of a breathtaking sunset, it felt as if it had been conjured by magic from another realm.

That wasn't too far from the truth. Thousands of unique talents, all masters of art and architecture, had put this place together. And from what she'd seen of its interior, modern magicians of technology had imbued it with the ultimate in luxury and functionality, too.

Approaching the palace from its shore-facing side took her through street-wide paths paved in earth-colored cobblestones and lined by soaring palm trees and flower beds. She strode through gates, courtyards, pavilions, everything bearing the intricacies and influences of the cultures that had melded together to form Judar. If she'd been in any-thing approaching a normal frame of mind, she would have savored the magnificence of this place. But now the majesty that surrounded her—and what it signified of her royal connections and their current implications for her life—oppressed her.

Scaling the convex stone steps that converged like a fan from a hundred feet at the bottom to thirty at the top, she gazed up at the massive palace that soared on four levels, echoing every hue of the desert, topped by a complex system of domes covered in mosaics and gold finials.

As she approached the entrance, two footmen in ornate uniforms seemed to materialize out of nowhere to open the twenty-foot mahogany double doors inlaid with gold and silver.

Smiling at them or offering thanks was useless, since they looked firmly ahead, avoiding eye contact. She crossed into the circular columned hall that had to be at least two hundred feet in diameter with a ceiling dome at least half that.

Her gaze swam around the superbly lit sweeping spaces, getting only impressions of neutral color schemes and sumptuous decor and furnishings. Again it felt deserted. Or everyone was giving her space. Which was very welcome. She didn't want to meet anyone right now, even in passing.

At the end of the hall, she entered an elevator that transported her in seconds to her fourth-floor quarters.

As she entered the expansive three-chambered wing and crossed to the bedroom, the sensory overload of sweet incense and opulence hit her. Yearning for her simple, cozy, two-room American abode twisted inside her like a tornado.

"Oh, you're here!"

The bright exclamation had her swinging around, almost severing her already compromised balance.

Aliyah. Kamal's wife and her queen. And a more fitting queen she'd never seen. As a former model, Aliyah was even taller than Jala, but now boasted the lush curves of a woman who'd ripened with the passion of a virile man, and with bearing his son and daughter. Her mahogany hair was in a thick braid over her shoulder, and she was swathed in a floor-length dress the color of her chocolate eyes.

She had Carmen with her. As Farooq's wife, Carmen was the crown prince's consort and yet another specimen of feminine gorgeousness, looking like a statuesque Rita Hayworth in her garnet-haired period but with turquoise eyes. Farah, the wife of her second-oldest brother, Shehab, was the only one missing. Shehab called her his Emerald Fairy for her eyes, and in Jala's opinion he was right all around, and Farah was the most ethereally stunning of the three.

If she'd cared about her looks, Jala would have suffered serious insecurity in the presence of those three visions. As it was, she was delighted her brothers had found women who were as beautiful on the outside as they were on the inside and who adored them. It was always such a pleasure to see them. Even though their relationship consisted mostly of video chatting, since the three couples seldom left Judar due to their growing families and responsibilities.

"We did knock." Carmen grinned at her apologetically as she beckoned the four women who accompanied her and Aliyah, no doubt their ladies-in-waiting. All were laden with packages. "We assumed you weren't here when you didn't answer, and thought to leave you the stuff with a note."

"We brought you everything we could think of to see what you need and what fits," Aliyah explained.

Carmen smiled at the women who'd piled the "stuff" in the sitting area, then gestured for them to leave. "Kamal said you need everything since you left New York without packing a thing."

"Yeah, because he told me your husband was lying in hospital battling the grim reaper."

Carmen blanched, the very idea of that evidently making her sick to her stomach. "He *what?*"

"*Exactly* what I said to him when he revealed that it was only a ruse to get me here."

"*Ya Ullah!*" Aliyah groaned, looking mortified. "I'll brain him for you. If you haven't already."

"I only let him live for you and the kids," Jala mumbled.

Aliyah hugged her, contrite on her husband's behalf. "I'm *so* sorry. He's a colossal pain but…" She sighed, eyes becoming dreamy. "I let him live because he's so utterly irresistible."

Jala knew exactly what she meant. *She* was caught, again, in the web of such an inexorable force. Just not happily so.

"You're talking to the world's second foremost expert on Kamal, regrettably my so-called twin and now horrifically my king, too. I am thinking of surrendering my Judarian nationality so I'd deprive him of wielding that kind of power over me."

"As if anyone can make you do anything you don't want." Carmen's scoff was certainty itself.

Farooq's wife had once told Jala she thought her the strongest, most courageous and independent person she knew. If only Carmen knew that there was someone who'd always made Jala do whatever *he* wanted. Was still making her do it.…

"Listen, we know you must be dying for an early night, so we won't keep you." Carmen linked her arm in Jala's.

"Let's open everything, and we'll see what suits you, what you need changed and what we forgot."

Aliyah followed them. "When Kamal said we should leave you alone all day, since you had a big day yesterday, I had no idea how big it was. No thanks to him. Giving you the scare, then the surprise of your life in succession."

"He told you, huh?" Jala huffed. "What am I *saying?* I think he tells you stuff before he tells it to himself."

Aliyah's exquisite face lit up with that expression of a woman secure in her power over her man, of his total love, which she reciprocated to her last breath. "He does think aloud with me. But not this time. I was told after the fact."

"After he settled the pact to sign me over in marriage to the future king of Jareer, you mean? To stop a war that old goat king of Saraya wouldn't think twice about instigating?"

Aliyah whooped. "Kamal calls him 'old goat,' too. You two really are twins!"

Carmen chuckled. "We heard you met said future king of Jareer last night. With how things are between Judar and Saraya, we never had the pleasure, but we've been hearing all sorts of things about him…like he's materialized right out of *Arabian Nights*. I've even heard women here make blasphemous comments about him—that he's even more impressive than *our* men."

Even loving her brothers as she did, Jala had to agree. Regretfully. She didn't know if it was better or worse to get more confirmation that he affected all women the same way.

Suddenly she jumped.

Carmen started. "What is it?"

Groaning, Jala got her phone out of her pocket. "Just my phone. It never vibrated that hard." Or she had surplus electricity coursing through her system. "Just a sec."

She cast a look at the number as she answered. A

blocked one. Probably one of her colleagues that the service provider here was unable to show on caller ID due to the international number.

"I am here."

She lurched harder this time. *Mohab.*

Here? Where? In her wing? Outside in the sitting room…?

"In the palace."

Oh.

"Are you in your quarters?"

She snatched a look at Carmen and Aliyah, who'd turned their backs, giving her privacy. "Yes."

"Where is it?"

"Why?"

"I plan on visiting you."

"And I plan on not receiving you."

"*Zain.* Turn on your laptop."

"Huh?"

"I'll have to improvise. Making love to you across cyberspace isn't ideal, but it might be a good idea to keep my distance until I take the edge off…the first few times."

Her knees almost buckled. "Why don't you go ahead on your own? Cyberspace is full of…material you can help yourself to."

She saw Carmen's back stiffen. It was imperceptible, but she'd heard her. And no doubt understood.

And that royal bastard continued to pour more dark magic into her inflamed brain. "I'm very fastidious about the…material…I help myself to. I have a specific movie that I have…helped myself to, times beyond count. I've long memorized every frame, had remastered it for better image and sound quality so I can help myself to it… into infinity."

A movie. Of her. As he'd massaged her, pampered her,

owned her every inch, brought her to ecstasy over and over again before he'd mounted her and thrust her to oblivion.

It had been one of her deepest scars, knowing that she'd trusted him so much she'd allowed this, that he had that evidence of her stupidity and self-destructiveness, a weapon to wield against her to serve his purposes.

"I would do anything for new material." His voice dropped an octave into the darkest reaches of temptation. "*Anything,* Jala." He let out a ragged breath that all but fried her synapses. "Turn on your laptop and we'll proceed."

She ground her teeth, refusing to press her legs together. He wasn't doing this to her, and over the phone, too, with her sisters-in-law feet away. "So I turn my laptop on and you magically see me from yours?"

"You keep forgetting who I am."

"You can tap into my computer?" she snapped.

"Of course. But I don't need to now. I just need to know your chat login. Which I do. Now hurry. The longer you make me wait, the longer before I'm appeased. I'm already half out of my mind with keeping my hands off you last night."

"You did no such thing!"

Her exclamation made both Aliyah and Carmen fidget. They must now be formulating a very good idea of what was going on.

Ya Ullah...she hated him!

"You know I did." He did that thing again with his voice that strummed the chords in the core of her being. "You know what I do with my hands when I don't keep them off you. But I kept something on. Your clothes. I almost had a heart attack needing to peel them off you. Take them off for me now, Jala. I want to see you now, want to imagine my hands on you. Show me yourself, *ya jameelati.*"

Ya Ullah—even now, he had her spontaneously combusting from a distance. Her body was readying itself, the clothes he'd asked her to remove were suddenly suffocating shackles, abrading aching flesh.

"I have company."

"Get rid of them." His command was terse, tense, uncompromising.

"I can't," she choked, smiling wanly at the two ladies who'd finished unpacking and were fidgeting, not knowing what to do. "I'm hanging up now."

"Do that, and I'll come over."

"You don't know where I am!"

"I can pinpoint your location via GPS. I was only asking as a courtesy, so you'd volunteer it willingly."

"What do you think I can do now, huh?"

"Would you have done what I asked had you been alone?"

Carmen strode by her to usher in the ladies, who brought in more packages, looking relieved to stop pretending to be talking to Aliyah and not hearing everything Jala said.

Jala cast her a brittle smile, trying to sound neutral as she almost choked on her answer. "I would have considered it."

"Liar." This was crooned in the darkest, deepest tone he'd ever hit her with. "You would have made a protracted feast of tormenting me."

That coming from the master of torment. Oh, the irony.

"*Zain*. If you can't open your laptop, we'll use the phone. I'll show you myself, instead."

Her legs gave out. She groped for the nearest chair, gesturing weakly at the ladies that she was okay, hoping they'd just leave. They didn't. They continued to work until she almost screamed she wanted to be alone to deal with this nerve-racking man without having them witness her being seduced out of her mind by him.

Mohab droned on until she felt her brain sizzling. "Remember how you used to revel in exposing me? Taking each shred of clothes off me with fingers that shook with urgency, with teeth that chattered with arousal?"

"Mohab..."

As soon as his name moaned out of her, begging mercy, she could almost see Aliyah's and Carmen's ears pricking up. Now they knew for sure who'd been tormenting her all this time.

"But I'll leave you to your visitors on one condition."

"What?" she croaked.

"The moment they're gone, you'll come to me."

To their credit, after Mohab released her from his long-distance torture, Aliyah and Carmen behaved as if they'd heard nothing as they concluded their business, which it turned out they *had* needed to stay to conclude. Before they disappeared, she thought she saw them exchanging furtive smiles.

Yeah. They were probably putting two and two together. And coming up with a thousand.

She took her time, showering, drying her hair, dressing in fresh clothes. Then she headed to the wing Mohab had been given. Aliyah had backhandedly provided its location.

At his door, she knocked, then stood back.

The door opened almost instantaneously. Across the threshold, there he was, looking fall-to-your-knees gorgeous—*Mohab*.

In a black-on-black suit and shirt, his skin simmered and his eyes glowed in the soft ambient light. Only the top section of his hair was held back now; the rest flowed like thick sheets of silk to sigh over his collar.

A wave of fierce hunger rolled over her. She bore its impact without any outward sign, looking up at him across the threshold. He only stepped aside. Knowing there'd be eyes documenting her entry into his chambers, she walked inside.

The wing looked much like the one she occupied, but it smelled different. His scent had already permeated the place. It coated her lungs, tingled on her tongue. His unique brand of virility and vigor, of scorching desert sun and flaying wind, of ruthless terrain and cleansing rain. Of cold-blooded termination and boiling-over passion.

His appreciation sizzled over her as his eyes swept her white-cotton-clad body, sensuality playing on his sculpted lips, humming from him like electricity from a high-voltage cable.

She bore the brunt of his silent, sensual onslaught, then, in utmost tranquillity and premeditation, she swung her arm and socked him in the jaw.

Six

Pain exploded in Jala's hand.

She'd thrown punches before, but nothing had ever hurt that bad. Figured. Mortal beings' jaws weren't made of some indestructible amalgam like *Arabian Nights* refugee here.

She might have broken her hand. And wrist. And elbow.

But she wouldn't obey the need to shake the agony out and howl. The unmovable bastard hadn't even rocked under what she'd thought a very good punch. Only his smile had vanished, his expression becoming that of a predator who'd just encountered an unexpected opponent, exhilarated by the discovery, raring for an all-out tumble.

Then, oh, so slowly, he raised his hand and rubbed his jaw, softly scratching against his beard. It sent a frisson of stimulation through her, as if those fingers had scraped against her most sensitive spots. She managed not to shudder.

"Was that so hard?"

Huh? What?

"Giving me that first voluntary touch." He rubbed his jaw again, this time moving it from side to side, as if making sure everything was still slotted in place and functioning. "Not bad at all, as first voluntary touches go."

Wishing she could generate heat vision, she glared at him. "If only you'd told me you expected a first voluntary *punch,* I would have obliged you much faster."

His grin turned into a wince and back to a grin. "Good thing I'm sporting a beard. I would have had a hard time explaining the bruise. That *was* a perfect jab. Or should I say, sucker punch?"

"*Please.* You saw it coming a light-year away. You could have blocked it if you wanted."

"If you think I saw anything but you glowing like a golden goddess in that torture device of a dress, you give me too much credit. You reduce me to my basic beast and the most simpleminded and oblivious of men."

Why was he *doing* this? Reengaging his seduction program? Was there something he still needed from her? Was he making sure she was hot enough for the required malleability?

"At least believe that if I'd seen this punch coming, I would have ducked so you wouldn't hurt your hand."

"Oh, sure. You care about the hand that just socked you."

"I care about nothing *but* your every bone and pore and inch. All I want is to show you how much…I care. But wait…"

He suddenly turned and strode away, disappeared into the kitchenette. In moments, he came back with a bag of ice. Stopping before her, he took her hand, ran gentle fingers over the knuckles that throbbed with a dull ache, his eyebrows knotting as he examined the forming bruise.

Placing the ice on her knuckles, he gritted his teeth, as if her gasp hurt him.

"Next time, use a heavy, blunt object."

A shudder rattled through her, at his dark mutter more than at the icy numbing. She'd known she'd pay the price for her recklessness in pain and limited mobility for a while. But she'd thought it a small price for venting her frustration in the one way she hadn't tried yet. Physically.

She only felt worse now—stupid on top of out-of-control and futile. And his solicitude had turned the tables on her. She'd known he wouldn't retaliate, but she'd hoped it would surprise him into baring his fangs, or at least dropping his mask. He'd done that once, that night six years ago.

She'd always conjured those moments when he'd snarled at her like a wounded beast, when unstoppable longing for him had almost snuffed her will to go on. But even then, he'd exposed her to the full range of his faces. Passionate, anxious, shocked, angry, possessive, bewildered and betrayed. Thinking none of those had been real had only made her unable to trust her judgment again. Just as she couldn't now.

Carefully removing the ice, he lifted her hand to his lips. Holding her eyes as if he wanted her to let him into her soul, he feathered each knuckle with a kiss that was tender, almost reverent. And something in the center of her being buckled.

For him to be kissing the hand that had just inflicted an act of aggression and affront on him was too much. Unsteadily, she withdrew her hand.

He exhaled, flexed his hand as if it hurt, too, before it went up to the side of his neck.

Then he suddenly grinned at her. "What do you know... you fixed my neck!"

The spontaneity of his grin, the ease, the *warmth,* how real this all felt—her longing for the man she'd once loved with every fiber of her being—suddenly overwhelmed her. The yearning that had writhed inside her like a burning serpent lurched so hard that her nails dug into her good hand's palm until they almost broke her skin.

"Okay. You achieved your purpose, made sure my sisters-in-law heard the kind of conversation you forced on me…."

His hand rose in protest. "How could I have known they were with you?"

"Because you apparently keep me under surveillance every second I'm awake, maybe even when I'm asleep."

"I told you I didn't know where you were."

"Even if I believe this, I told you I had company. In fact, having anyone else present would have been even more damaging. But you established what you wanted. That our relationship goes far beyond last night, and its past nature is also implicit if you could talk to me with such… audacity."

"How could they have known I was being…audacious?"

"Because your phone seduction session made my responses clear to anyone who knows anything about sexual innuendo. So—you've established my 'impurity' and your role in it. Now, even if I want to back down, it will be at the cost of disgracing my family, now that my 'shame' is out. While you will keep the high moral ground, even if you're the once defiler of my honor, since you're here now doing the honorable thing."

He coughed an incredulous laugh. "Where are you getting all this? If you believe your sisters-in-law suspect anything, and it disturbs you, I'll take care of it. I started my 'phone seduction' before I knew you weren't alone, and I didn't continue it because of any of the motives you assign me. You're crediting me with a premeditation I already told you I'm incapable of around you."

Feeling her head would burst with frustration, she began

to turn away when a cabled arm slipped around her waist, clasping her to his formidable length. "I was up all night, Jala, every inch of me *roaring* for you. I let you go last night because I thought I must give you some breathing room. But my resolutions vanished the moment I got here. All I could think was that you were near, and all I planned was having you, and this time not letting you walk away. As you did last night. As you did six years ago."

She pushed out of his arms. "You can stop doing this."

"I can't. I can never stop wanting you."

"I mean it, Mohab. Stop it. I already told you I'm going through with this charade. Now drop the seduction act."

The arms reaching for her stopped in midmotion, dropping to his sides. "What reason do you assign me for acting this time, if, according to you, I've already fulfilled my purpose?"

She shrugged, shoulders knotted, throat closing. "I never know anything where you're concerned."

"Didn't you say you know everything about my motivations and methods?" He shook his head. "Does this mean you didn't believe anything I said last night?"

She didn't know anymore. The dejection in his eyes, the intensity she felt from him, all added to the verdict of her senses. Even if she couldn't trust those, she couldn't disregard her observations.

His reaction to her punch had been seamless. If he'd been acting, he would have been resenting it—and her. It would have manifested in even momentary fury, in an instinctive spark of retaliation, before he curbed it. He'd only been astonished, and the instant hue of his surprise had been acceptance, indulgence, even elation. As if he'd meant it when he'd said he'd take anything from her, as if he welcomed any punishment she inflicted if it would vent her anger toward him.

She *could* be seeing what she wanted to see all over again, but she…

All her hairs stood on end. Something had slithered in the background, at ground level….

Her tension deflated on a squeaked exclamation. "A cat!"

She blinked at the magnificent creature. A robust white Turkish Angora, clearly just woken up from a sound catnap with the way it stopped to stretch and arch. Then it slunk toward them, languidly weaving its way around furniture.

"I wonder whose it is!" She turned incredulous eyes to Mohab. "Did you know it was here?"

Her eyes almost popped at the change that came over Mohab's expression as he looked at the cat. It was the tender delight she'd only seen on people's faces when they beheld their babies.

"I should hope so, since she's mine. Or should I say, I'm hers?" He bent as the cat approached him, tail straight up and trembling in the cat-tail-language equivalent of "I'm crazy about you," before rearing up on her hind legs like a baby asking to be picked up. Mohab obliged at once, scooping her up, cradling her expertly against his massive chest…and getting white fur all over his pristine black clothes.

Purring so loudly the sound vibrated in Jala's ears, the cat surrendered to Mohab's pampering as he cooed to her. "Who's awake? Who's had a good nap?"

She gaped at the incongruent scene. Mohab, that lethal juggernaut, all but melting over a cat.

Mohab had a cat.

As the knowledge hit bottom in her mind, another movement made her snap her gaze to the same direction where Whitey had come from, only to find more felines advancing.

He had *cats. Four* of them.

Or maybe there were more still napping in there. At this point, she would believe just about anything.

One of the cats, a miniature glossy-black panther, broke into a lope and threw himself at Mohab's feet. Then, butting his head against Mohab's legs, he made him widen his stance so he could weave between them in excited figure eights. The other two cats, a tabby Scottish Fold and a Russian Blue, soon joined in, purring the place down.

Mohab looked over at her when he had two cats in his arms, his expression that of a proud dad.

The tightness in her throat grew thorns. "Is this your... pride?"

"They are my pride and joy. They're my family."

The word *family* penetrated her heart, a shard that had never stopped driving deep.

He'd once told her his life story. He was an only child and, like her, both his parents were dead. But he hadn't lost them to illness or to heartbreak. He'd lost them—twelve years ago, now—in a terrorist attack. One meant for him.

Whenever she remembered that she'd used that knowledge to take a stab at him, she still choked with shame. It hadn't mattered that she'd been mad with agony—it had still been unforgivable. Some things should never be used as a weapon, no matter what. Should never be used at all. It had been dishonorable of her to use such an intimate and painful injury against him.

It never ceased to torment her that she owed him that much. Her life, and an apology for that cruel transgression. But since she'd thought she'd never settle those debts with him, she'd added them to her forward payment to the world.

But he'd invoked her debt last night. Then there'd been everything else. And just when she thought she was confused enough about him, she discovered he had cats!

She found herself asking, "You travel with them?"

He bent down, gently letting both cats jump lithely from his embrace. "People travel with their kids, don't they?"

The way he said that tightened her throat more. "You never told me you liked cats. Or that you had any."

Straightening, he approached her with a stealthy grace, like a huge version of the felines, his eyes radiating this new warmth that seeped to her core. "I didn't then. I've always loved cats, all animals for that matter, but my lifestyle made me unable to adopt any. In my previous post, I had no control over my schedule. After I resigned—and after I settled a...personal project that took me all over the world five years ago—I set up my own business. Then I got my beauties, here—all rescue kitties, each with a story of her or his own." Suddenly his expression changed, as if something disturbing had just occurred to him. "You don't like cats?"

Her heart thudded at the alarm in his eyes. "I'm *crazy* about them. I had three cats when I lived in Judar, but I lost them all before I left. I fostered only in the States, since my globe-trotting lifestyle wouldn't accommodate a cat. Unlike you, I don't have my own private jet to haul them along with me."

His smile broke out again. "Let's test this claim, shall we? My darlings are cat-lover detectors. We'll let them scan you, but be advised...their verdict is final and incontestable."

He might be joking, but she was anxious they might snub her. Why, she didn't know. She was doing her best to alienate him, so why did she wish to appeal to his "kids"?

She swallowed the contrary lump of nervousness. "How will you know they approve of me?"

"How do cats show approval?"

"Each cat has his or her own way of showing it."

"Exactly." He flashed her a sizzling smile as he prowled to the sitting area, took off his jacket, dropped it to the ground and let his cats walk over it. "I should have changed into something light colored as soon as I let them out of the carriers. Only Rigel goes with this outfit."

His shoulders seemed to widen as he slowly started to unbutton his black shirt. Her heart stuttered. He was stripping.

She could swear the silk slithered off his skin with an aching sigh, as if it hated to separate from his flesh. She knew just how it felt, remembered how her hands used to ache for the time when they could glide all over him.

As his formidable back was exposed, symmetry and perfection made into a symphony of muscle and sinew, her salivary glands gushed. She was literally drooling over him.

At the damask burgundy couch in the center of the sitting area he turned to her, giving her a full frontal assault.

He was even more magnificent than she remembered. His chest had broadened, his abdomen had become more defined, every bulge and slope harder, packing more power, every line chiseled by endless stamina and determination. Her breasts swelled, reliving nights of abandon writhing beneath that chest, her stomach clenched with the memory of that ridged abdomen bearing down on her, working her into a frenzy. Her core throbbed with the moist heat that had been simmering since he'd walked into that stateroom.

Then in one of those movements that made her want to devour every glorious inch of him, he sank down on the couch.

Spreading his bulk over the cushions, he braced his legs wide apart and caressed the couch on both sides. The invitation was for his cats this time, who zoomed to obey, climbing all over him, butting their heads against every part of him, jumping on the back of the couch so they could reach his face and rub and kiss and lick him all over it. He surrendered to their love with a look of bliss, his eyes fixing her in a steady barrage of seduction.

Before this, he was the most overwhelming man to her, just by existing. Now this was…cruel. This had to be the most mind-bending thing he'd ever exposed her to. The sight of him, surrounded by cats, letting them plumb the depths of his love, roaming all over him in total trust and affection.

Did that man want to blow her ovaries?

He caught the ginger Scottish Fold who was crossing his lap and deposited a kiss on his head. "This is Mizar… as you can see why." She certainly could. The tomcat was a magnificent tabby with the cutest white apron in history. Mohab put him down to answer the impatience of the Russian Blue as she asked for her turn. "And this is Nihal. She is addicted to water taps, so I have to leave her a trickle on all the time. Always a challenge on flights." Nihal meant thirst quenching, so very appropriate, too. After she took her turn in her "daddy's" embrace she moved on and Mohab turned to the little panther. "And this is Rigel. I bet you know why I called him that."

She sure did. *Rigel* meant foot, and Rigel was definitely a foot cat, the one who'd hurled himself at Mohab's feet. Actually Rigel, the star, meant The Foot of the Great One, which was very apt for both cat and owner.…

Hey…wait! "These are all star names, ones discovered by ancient astronomers from the region."

Surprise flared in his eyes. "They *are* my little stars. Very observant…and knowledgeable of you."

Pleasure revved inside her stomach. She'd once craved his praise, praise he'd lavished on her, that had made her feel like the most special person in the world. So even in that regard, nothing had changed.

"And this is Sette—my mistress and queen of my household." The white cat jumped on his lap, curled up and rested her head on his thigh, eyes focused in the distance. Mohab swept her in strokes, making Jala feel his hand running down *her* back. "But *you* can be my human mistress and queen."

Queen. She still couldn't get her head around the fact that Mohab wasn't just a prince anymore. Or just a major force in the world of extragovernmental crisis management. He would have his own throne. And if she married him, she'd be his queen.

Which couldn't happen. He would have to look for someone else to...

The thought lodged into her brain like a red-hot ax.

How dog in the manger was that? She wouldn't be his, and she couldn't bear completing a thought where another woman was?

But that wasn't new. She'd spent years shying away from any thoughts along these lines, always keeping her mind in a fever of preoccupation so she'd never focus on images of Mohab with other women, when he must have had scores....

"Won't you proceed with our test?"

His soft question severed her oppressive musings. Feeling any sudden movement would collapse her to the ground, she started toward him. The moment she moved, all four cats seemed to suddenly take notice of her, ears pricking, bodies in attention mode, eyes fixing her with the same intensity as their daddy's.

She came down on the far end of the couch, taking care not to touch any of the cats. Mizar was the first one who approached, sniffing her tentatively. She'd missed having a cat so much, all she wanted was to grab his robust body and bury her face in his thick fur.

Reeling back the urge, she gave Mizar her hand to sniff, cooing to him, "*Ma ajmalak ya sugheeri*...do you know how beautiful you are, my little one?" Mizar answered by bonking her hand with his head. Her heart trembled with this affection it only reserved for animals. "Oh, you do know exactly how delightful you are, you compact package of joy, you!"

The cat made his decision and climbed onto her lap, reaching up to bump his head into her chin.

She giggled, everything emptying from her mind but the delight cats always engendered in her. "*Ya Ullah*...you magical creature. I had a ginger boy like you once, but without your apron. He was as sweet as you and I miss him so very much...."

Hot needles pricked behind her eyes, dissolved in moist pain that she'd thought she'd expended so many years ago.

Needing to hide it from Mohab, she picked up Mizar and buried her face in his nape. A prod on her shoulder came from her side. It was Nihal, asking to be introduced. She turned to the cat, offering her hand. But Nihal, having seen Mizar already on her, dispensed with preliminaries and climbed down Jala's arm to arch and rub against her side and then settle down against her thigh, a front leg draped over it. Rigel jumped from the couch, sniffed her feet first, then jumped up and joined the lap-warming party. At last, Sette rose regally from Mohab's lap and sashayed over, pushing Mizar out of the way in the center of Jala's lap and making the spot hers.

Distributing strokes, delighting in their softness and trust, heart dancing to the frequency of their purrs, Jala looked at Mohab, her smile unfettered for the first time since...her days with him. "This is the best way to die, drowning in cats!"

He didn't smile back. Before her smile faltered, Mohab rose quietly, came to stand before her, his legs brushing hers as she sat covered in his cats. Then he came down on his knees before her.

Her breath left her in a choking gasp as he leaned forward, his hands brushing her heavy, aching breasts as his arms slid behind her. "You didn't only pass, *ya jameelati,* you broke my cat's fastidiousness and suspiciousness barrier in record time. They didn't even take to me that fast. It's official, they have marked you as a bona fide cat slave."

Her smile broke out again, wavering this time. He bore down on her, this time making his cats vacate her lap and rearrange themselves around her. He pressed himself between her legs, making her open them for him, bringing him fully against her, the hard flesh of his bare chest burning through her dress, his harder arousal pressing into the junction of her thighs. She watched his face approaching hers with the same fatalism one would give an approaching train.

"How about *living* drowning in cats?" His lips landed on her jaw, nuzzled its way up to her ear. "I and my family are all yours for the taking, *ya jameelati.* So take us."

This was so…incredible an offer it would have been everything she'd want from life if it had been real and only for her. If it had been in another life where the past and its losses hadn't taken place. This way, it was just more pain.

Her useless arms pushed against him. "I said I will *say* I'll marry you, not that I will."

He gathered her closer again. "And I will take anything you're willing to give. If you won't marry me, even temporarily, you can still be with me. You can still have me."

"You expect me to sweep everything under the rug and just fall into your arms again?"

"Under the rug is where all the irrelevant crap of the past belongs. And in my arms is where you do."

Her senses leaped so hard she felt as if they'd tear out of the confines of her body. All they'd ever wanted was to smother themselves in his nearness, his pleasures. Damn them. And damn him. Pulling her strings, dangling himself, reminding her how it had felt to be mingled with his flesh, riding his need, drenched in pleasure, inundated with satisfaction.

"You and *Al Shaitaan* are closely related, aren't you?" She exhaled. "Forget that. The devil must come to you for conniving lessons." And temptation and seduction ones. "You must be his chief consultant."

He just smiled. And why not? He felt her buckling.

She'd be damned if she did again, when he'd already condemned her to six years of misery. She wasn't letting hormones run amok again, wouldn't let them suppress her self-preservation.

"Why are you *doing* this?"

"Because it's the only thing I *can* do, *ya ameerati al jameelah.* I've starved for you and I'll do anything so I can sate myself with you again."

She stared into his eyes and again could only *feel* his sincerity. As if whatever else hadn't been right, this was the one thing that had always been real…his desire for her.

Years of damaged self-worth and disbelief in her judgment trembled one last time…then everything shattered.

As if feeling the second it did, his arms tightened, bringing her colliding with his steely mass, his lips taking hers and swallowing her moan of surrender.

Then she found herself being plucked up by his momentum as he pitched backward on the lush Persian carpet, sprawled over it and stretched her on top of him. She vaguely felt the cats jumping after them, felt them prodding, as if to make sure they were okay.

Cradling her head in his large palms, Mohab turned his to his cats. "I'm going to make love to Jala now, so go eat or bathe or something. We won't have time for you for a while."

As if they understood him, the cats slunk away.

Turning his attention back to her, he pulled her down, had her lips sinking into his and her core on his erection. He rocked against her, promising her, deluging her in readiness. Coherence dissolved on his invading tongue, drowned in his taste, her senses igniting like firecrackers with every plunge, sweep and groan....

Remember what he cost you. The havoc he'd still wreak if you surrender. And you still *didn't contest your main gripe.*

Feeling as if she'd left a layer of skin stuck to his hot lips and hands, she scrambled off him, getting to her feet clumsily before plopping on the couch again.

Brooding with hunger, radiating it, he rose to his elbows, stretching before her half-naked like a god of abandon.

Before she crawled back over him, she bit her tingling lips. "So I got this part. You want me. Fine. How about we discuss another concern? Your transgressions?"

He was on his feet in what should have been an impossible movement. She was in good shape herself, but this was a level of fitness and strength that was almost scary.

His lips twisted. *"Ma gatalnahom bahthann baad?"*

Haven't we already killed them with investigation? The regional expression for draining a topic of life.

She nodded, still shaky. "The old ones. But with you, there's always new ones." She sucked in a burning stream of aggravation. "You spied on me. You evidently still do."

"I tried to stop. I couldn't."

So simple. So stymieing. Why couldn't she do herself the life-saving favor of not wanting him anymore?

He threw himself down beside her, grimacing. "That's not true. I *didn't* try. I knew I couldn't stop watching over you." Head resting on the couch, he turned his face toward her, inches from her own. "Jala, we both try to save the world in our own ways. But I'm the one who's versed in its dangers, who can take measures to eradicate them. I won't apologize for keeping tabs on you. You lead a very dangerous life."

"I do social and humanitarian work!"

"In the world's most dangerous places. Apart from the damages that could befall anyone just being there, you're a temptation to even the most harmless of men."

She gaped at him.

"It's bigger than me, Jala, the need to know you're safe. And since I'm the one best equipped to keep you safe, I do."

Incredulity burst out of her. "*I* keep me safe."

For a split second, his eyes said she knew nothing.

This brought her sitting up. "Are you telling me you saved me from a danger I was unaware of?"

Another blip said he'd saved her from far more than *a* danger. But he just shook his head. "Just leave it. I wasn't 'spying' on you. I was reassuring myself of your safety and making sure you were safe. There's a big difference."

The lump that now inhabited her throat again grew harder.

Believing this would change so much. Mean too much. And she couldn't handle more changes of perspective right now. The foundations of her existence, as miserable as they'd been, had constituted her stability. Losing them all, having to erect so many new ones so suddenly, was too…overwhelming. And he was already enough on his own.

In defense, she groped for one of her established suspicions. "Or you were afraid I'd go after Najeeb again?"

He huffed a mirthless laugh. "And what would I have done if you did? I believed you'd gone to him when you left me, and there was nothing I could do about it." At her glower, he ground out, "I *didn't* tell him anything."

She had no idea why, but this time, she believed him.

Yet another pillar knocked over.

After a moment in which he seemed to debate the wisdom of divulging another piece of the puzzle, he said, "I only found out later why Najeeb cut all ties with you."

And he told her why. At least what he believed to be true. *She* knew the real reason why Najeeb hadn't contacted her again. Because she wouldn't let him. But Mohab believed King Hassan's slandering had ended her relationship with Najeeb.

After discovering King Hassan had been behind her ordeal in the past, and knowing he was now the reason behind this current crisis, she didn't feel bad about not exonerating him from *that* specific crime. It hadn't been for lack of trying that he wasn't guilty of it after all.

Mohab was continuing, "Then you disappeared, and I couldn't find you for months. When you resurfaced, there was no way I was going to let you out of my sight again."

She let out her bated breath. "If I say I believe you, you have to promise to stop."

He must have gauged they'd entered the negotiation zone as he bore down on her again, deluging her in a fresh wave of temptation. "Why? Who wouldn't want a guardian angel like me? I'm very handy, you know. People pay me tens of millions to keep them safe. I am offering you a free ride for life."

His arms were halfway around her when she pushed out of them again and stood up, teetering with the urge to throw herself back into them, come what may. But this was just too soon, too fast…too much. She needed to slow down, take a look at where she was jumping, before she plunged into the deep end…again.

Groaning, he stood up as well, his eyes suddenly totally serious for the first time since she'd seen him again. "I've told you the truth about everything so far. All but one thing."

Her breath deserted her as she turned fully toward him.

Looking as if he was dragging shrapnel from his own flesh, he rasped, "You don't have to marry me...or even say you would. You can leave right now, and there'd be no war."

Seven

Mohab met his own eyes in the steamed-up mirror and reached a conclusion. He was insane.

He'd gotten Jala to agree to a fake engagement, then progressed to alleviate her every doubt about the sincerity of his desire. Her surrender to his lovemaking, her mind-blowing response, had admitted her equal need. Her capitulation had only been a matter of time. If he'd just kept his mouth shut, he might have had her in his bed again by now.

But he hadn't kept his mouth shut.

Mizar and Sette rubbed against his legs, distracting him from wanting to bash himself over the head.

Sighing, he picked them up and headed out of the bathroom with Nihal and Rigel weaving between his legs. Even they couldn't make him feel better now. They actually made him feel worse. All they did was remind him of his pleasure at Jala's delight in them, of how it had felt to share them with her.

Topping up their treats in the kitchenette, he told them

he needed to be alone. As usual, they understood him and gave him space, not following him to the wing's reception chamber.

He stood in the middle of the magnificent space Kamal had bestowed on him and could still barely believe he was actually here. An Aal Ghaanem treated as an honored guest in the Aal Masood stronghold. A week ago, that would have been the material of a ridiculous joke. But Kamal had been given a second chance with his queen and was making a real effort to pay it forward.

And what had *he* done with all of Kamal's support and all the ground he'd managed to gain with Jala? He'd voluntarily blown it all to hell.

He could still see Jala standing across from him, her face a frozen mask after he'd divulged that last bit of truth. Then she'd said one word.

"Explain."

He had. He'd told her everything, hadn't left out one single detail this time. After he'd finished, she'd just turned and walked out of his quarters.

That had been three days ago. She'd left the palace that same night. He'd thought she'd head straight to the airport and fly out of Judar, never to return. But her security detail had called to report that she'd checked into a hotel on the other side of Durgham. Moving all the way across the capital had been a clear message that she'd wanted to distance herself from the palace. And him. Trying to call her had yielded no results. She wasn't answering anyone's phone calls. Then she'd turned her phone off. And it was all his fault.

Exhaling forcibly, he moved to the French doors, stared sightlessly at the palace grounds. He had to face the fact that he couldn't have done anything else.

He'd lied to her too much during their relationship, hidden too much. At first believing he had to, then fearing the consequences of exposure. Then he'd seen her again, and she'd given him the full disclosure he'd long craved. And he'd realized that, apart from her own hang-ups about intimacy and commitment, the real reason he'd lost her all those years ago was because he hadn't been honest with her. After realizing that, he could hide nothing anymore. He'd wanted her to want him based on full disclosure, too, needed to have her this time in total honesty.

But after he'd confessed everything about the past, about his feelings, only one thing had remained. Her total freedom of choice about whether to be with him or not. So he'd given it to her.

And she'd chosen not to be with him.

The only reason he'd stayed in Judar till now was because she had. According to Farooq and Shehab, the ones she'd let near, having ostracized Kamal as well, she'd stayed only to see their kids a few times before she left. But she wouldn't remain in the palace where both the perpetrators of this latest deception resided. It was probably a matter of a couple days before she left. It would be over then.

Who was he kidding? It was *already* over. It had been over the minute she'd realized she didn't have to put up with seeing him again. And it didn't matter if she still wanted him. To Jala, freedom and autonomy and honesty had always mattered far more than her desires, no matter how ferocious those were.

A growl of exasperation burst from his depths. Enough. He'd set up an elaborate gamble to resolve this need for her that continued to eat at him, and he'd lost. Everything had depended on being able to win her, and he'd done so fleetingly, before he'd lost her again…big-time.

But he hadn't lost her because he'd told her the full truth—it was because he'd started this whole thing with another charade. He'd catastrophically miscalculated all over again. Seemed it was hopeless. Whenever it involved her, he, the master strategist, had once more been reduced to a bumbling idiot.

Growling again, unable to stay where she wasn't, he strode out of the wing.

He had to see Kamal before he left, tell him they'd have to plan another way to contain his uncle's wrath. As for Jala, he'd have to get her out of his system some other way....

"You're better than I gave you credit for. *Way* better."

Mohab squeezed his eyes shut as the deep, amused voice hit him between the shoulder blades.

His condition was much worse than he'd thought. He hadn't even felt Kamal approach.

What the hell. Get this over with.

He turned to Kamal…and almost winced. That was it. He no longer considered Kamal his new favorite person. This guy was just too happy. And it swamped Mohab with such…futility. A hopelessness that he'd ever feel anything like that.

"I was coming to see you…." he began.

Kamal took his arm. "I could have just called you, but I had to see you again and picture you in your future capacity, now that it has emerged from the realm of speculation to fact."

Mohab's frown deepened. He didn't get one word of what Kamal had just said.

Kamal went on, spouting more gibberish. "I really thought the next I heard from Jala would be with a proposal on how to avert the war without her involvement. And the worst part? Even if we'd been dealing with the original, critical situation, I had no doubt she'd present me with a real solution."

Kamal huffed a laugh at the word *solution,* which had evidently become an inside joke between them. However,

Mohab wasn't in any laughing mood over it, or over anything else, anymore.

Kamal continued, "She's been known to formulate workable solutions for some seemingly impossible situations to the satisfaction of all sides in some of the world's most volatile regions."

Mohab knew that. He'd followed her work closely, with the utmost interest and admiration. And more than a little humility and self-deprecation. For she'd been able, with far fewer resources and powers, to peacefully do what he'd thought could only be resolved through his extreme measures. And while he'd discreetly helped her wherever he could, he'd been honing his methods on her example.

But why was Kamal telling him all this now? Or was he the one who couldn't make sense of anything anymore?

Kamal, who'd taken him back to his quarters, was going on as they entered. "Then she leaves, and I think the next time I want to see her I'll have to chase after her on one of her jaunts around the world. But I should have known better than to predict Jala the Unpredictable. She left the palace only to go stay in a three-star hotel."

"I know that."

Kamal's fond expression deepened. "She was never one for luxury, but her work seems to have made her allergic to it. Not to mention her chronic independence issues. The eyes around here must have had her climbing walls. *Ya Ullah!*" His exclamation made Mohab blink. "I was told you brought cats, but I thought they mistook some other containers for carriers."

His cats were scurrying to welcome him back, slowing down to a curious, cautious prowl when they found he had company.

Grinning widely, Kamal bent to offer them his hands to sniff. "Four cats! There's no end to your surprises, Mohab, is there? Wait till my kids find out you have these beauties. You'll be their favorite uncle."

The word *uncle* stabbed him. He was destined not to be anyone's uncle. Anyone's anything. Seemed Kamal was still under the misapprehension that he might marry Jala.

Gritting his teeth, he watched his cats show Kamal the same level of instant trust and acceptance they'd shown Jala. Kamal probably *felt* the same as her to them, too.

Which was another reason he couldn't be around her brother any longer. "Listen, Kamal…"

Kamal straightened with Mizar in his arms, grinning. "I *do* want to listen—to just how you did it. I knew you were effective, but this borders on magic."

And Mohab had enough of all the ambiguity. "What the hell are you talking about?"

"I'm talking about Jala, of course. She just called me and told me to start the wedding preparations."

For the first time in his life, Mohab was totally in the dark.

Jala had told Kamal she would marry him.

Then, after Kamal had left, she'd called, making him certain he hadn't been hallucinating. She'd informed him that their "engagement" would be celebrated tomorrow over a family dinner.

He'd demanded to see her before said dinner, but she'd hung up without even a goodbye. He still wondered if he'd only listened to a prerecorded announcement.

Yet he couldn't care. This was his third, and probably final, chance—and he was not going to squander it this time.

To that end, he'd better get that wild-eyed look under control. Though the tuxedo-clad man who was reflected back at him in the ornate full-length mirror looked suave and polished, his expression was that of a starving wolf.

"I see why you didn't hear me knock. You're lost in admiring your own grandeur."

The soft mockery lashed him, had him swinging around. *Jala.*

She'd always been his ideal of femininity, the sum total of his fantasies, but tonight, she'd taken her sorcery to a new level. In an old-gold dress made of ethereal materials that wrapped her every curve to distressing advantage, she was overpowering...even otherworldly.

She headed for the open French doors and stopped with her back to him, contemplating the gardens at night. He approached her as if afraid she'd disappear if he made any sudden moves, and she looked at him over her shoulder with eyes as mysterious as Judar's night. Her hair sifted in the jasmine-laden night breeze with swishes that strummed his every nerve.

"You said you wanted to talk."

"Since you hung up on me, I didn't think you registered my request, or thought it not worth consideration."

"I reconsidered. We need to touch base before we face the combined forces of our families for the first time together."

He slid his arms around her, crisscrossed them beneath her breasts and pulled her back against his body. This was probably a damaging move right now. But he was beyond holding back. These past three days had been three days beyond the limits of his endurance.

Even though he felt her tense as he bent to breathe her in, she didn't resist. He went dizzy as the feel and scent and heat of her vitality and femininity eddied in his arteries.

"I thought I'd never see you again. Jala, *habibati*..."

He turned her in his arms and captured her lips with all his pent-up hunger and frustration.

Feeling her luscious mouth open beneath his, having his lungs fill with intoxication as she gasped a scorching

gust of passion, tore aside any semblance of moderation.
Bypassing all preliminaries, he plunged into her depths,
his tongue dueling with hers as he squeezed her against
him, his hands kneading down her body to bunch up the
chiffon layers of her skirt and seek the sizzling velvet of
her flesh. He dipped beneath the lace, cupping the perfection of her buttocks.

She tore her lips from his. "This isn't why I'm here…"

Gritting his teeth, he reluctantly let her go. If their engagement dinner wasn't less than half an hour away, he
would have convinced her otherwise.

It was still with utmost satisfaction that he watched her
hands tremble as she smoothed out the disarray created
by his passion. "I'm here to explain why I'm doing this."

"As long as you've reconsidered, I don't care why."

"You should, because I think you miscalculated."

Hah. Tell him about it. But she was probably referring
to some other miscalculation he was as yet unaware of.

"You think you can curb your uncle and dictate your
terms, resolving the crisis without my…participation. And
though I commend you for deciding to be forthright at last,
even when it was counterproductive to your other purposes, I believe you're wrong in thinking I'm not necessary to achieve your goal. You'd be right if we were talking
about someone other than your uncle. But with his track
record of paranoia and volatile pride he could still esca-
late the situation if Saraya's percentage doesn't appeal to
him, or if he feels slighted, even if it means going to war
against you, too."

"So what are you saying, exactly?" he asked carefully.

"That the marriage solution remains what he'd be most
likely to accept, the one that would save him face. If you
give him the added deference of being the one who puts
his hand in Kamal's, with both acting as our proxies, his
pride would bind him to peace from then on."

Kamal had been right. She was totally unpredictable. This was the last thing he'd expected her to do.

But there she was, doing exactly what Kamal had said she would. Coming up with a levelheaded and thorough analysis of the situation, based on her knowledge of all the players, and formulating the most workable solution. It again showed him he shouldn't have tried to manipulate her to seal the deal, should have come clean and hoped she'd make this offer on her own.

He inhaled. "That's extremely astute. And exceptionally thoughtful of you, to go to the effort of thinking this through so thoroughly and then agree to help, even after I tried to maneuver you into doing so under false pretenses."

Her strong shoulders jerked dismissively, causing her breasts to jiggle slightly and sending another rush of hormones roaring through him.

"Seems the first time is the worst. Then you get used to it." Before he could swear there'd be no more manipulation, she went on, "So anyway, I am your best bet, as you've already figured out, so I've decided to pitch in."

He pulled her back into his arms, meshing their gazes. *"Ashkorek, ya jameelati."*

She again pushed out of the circle of his arms. Story of his life from now on, it seemed.

"Don't thank me yet. I said this is what's most likely to get your uncle to cooperate, not that it's certain it will."

He shoved his hands into his pockets. "I don't care about the outcome. I only care about your intention."

She slanted him an unfathomable glance. "You seem to be in an uncaring mood today. Or is this your usual state? Probably." Another shoulder jerk. Another surge of lust. "You should start practicing caring. Being a king is quite a bit different from being a terminator."

"If anyone can teach me to care, it's you. As my queen."

Her gaze wavered. Was that…vulnerability?

Next split second it was gone, making him wonder if he'd even seen it.

"So about tonight…" she began.

No comment? Since she didn't intend to be his queen?

"What about it?"

"My sisters-in-law must have told my brothers their deductions about our relationship, based on your famous phone striptease session. Or, if by some miracle they managed some discretion, everyone must know by now that we're not strangers to each other. So how do you intend to play this in front of my family and yours?"

He raised her hands to his lips. "I intend to show everyone how proud I am to be your intended, that this was a hope I had harbored since I first saw you."

She withdrew her hands. "No need to go overboard, or you'll only make them suspicious."

She didn't believe him. Maybe because his statement was untrue. He *hadn't* thought of marriage in the years he'd craved her from afar, since he'd never thought marriage was in the cards for him at all. Even when he'd proposed, he had no picture of how marriage would fit into his existence.

But now, with the turn his life had taken, everything was different. Although he'd initially come here unclear about what he wanted, beyond the fact that he wanted her with a hunger that continued to consume him, he now wanted everything he could possibly have with her.

Her own stance seemed to be unchanged, though.

He had to hear her spell it out. "So your original agreement stands, as is?"

He held his breath. Hoping against hope…

Then she breathed, "Yes."

Eight

As soon as Mohab entered the expansive dining room in the king's quarters with Jala, the nine people seated at one end of the gigantic table stood up and clapped.

Mohab saw only one person. *Najeeb.*

Heat shot to his head. What was *he* doing here?

As per Jala's mandate, only the people necessary to the peace efforts should have been present. That had meant Kamal and his queen, Mohab's uncle and his queen and him and Jala.

He'd wholeheartedly welcomed that, had been enormously relieved when his uncle had begged off attending on account of illness. But to support Mohab's bid for the "incomparable Jala's" hand, King Hassan had promised to send her a priceless set of jewelry from Saraya's royal treasury.

It had been the ultimate irony to hear his uncle speaking in such glowing terms of the woman he'd once gone to dishonorable lengths to ensure didn't sully his royal family. Now that she was *the* princess of Judar, Hassan was embarrassingly eager to have her blood mingle with that of his family.

But Mohab had relaxed prematurely about tonight. King Hassan had sent Najeeb in his stead. Najeeb had also brought Jawad and Haroon, his second-oldest brothers among nine full and half siblings. But it was Najeeb's presence alone that disturbed Mohab. He'd avoided Najeeb for years, for every reason there was. A face-to-face with him, now of all times, topped the list of his least-favorite surprises ever. And he'd had some doozies in his time.

"Fi seh'hut al aroosain." Kamal raised a crystal glass filled with burgundy liquid, no doubt Judar's famous date wine, toasting the health of the bride- and groom-to-be.

Everybody raised their glasses and voices in salute, smiles of pleasure coating all faces. All faces but Najeeb's.

He didn't approve of this.

"So I had to do something as drastic as get engaged to end the Aal Masoods' and Aal Ghaanems' centuries-old theatrics, you testosterone-overdosed cavemen?"

General laughter rose in answer to Jala's humorous admonition as she smoothly unspooled from his loose embrace and entered the circle of welcome that opened for her. She was at once enfolded into the love and delight of her brothers and their wives. He envied them her readiness to go into their arms, to receive and return their kisses, to exchange smiles with them that were unmarred by the past.

Then she turned to his cousins, and his envy became resentment. Watching her bestow ease and humor on them actually hurt when he'd gotten nothing that approached either from her. When it brought back how it had felt to be inundated in both. It didn't help that those two hulking buffoons were totally enthralled as this magical creature welcomed them as friends and future family members.

Then it was Najeeb's turn.

He watched them approach each other with all the trepidation of someone watching a collision, one that would pulverize him. The hesitation of the long absence and the uncertainty of the other's reception evaporated with every step until they met halfway. Then she reached out both hands to him and he clasped them in his with just as much eagerness. But it was the tenderness on both their faces as their tentative smiles blossomed that had jealousy surging through him like a geyser. He felt that if he opened his mouth right now, he'd scorch the whole room.

He had no idea what he said to Jala's family as they gathered around to congratulate him. All he could see was Najeeb's head bent close to Jala's, making his blood boil.

"Take it easy, Mohab, or the guy might drop dead."

That was Shehab. Mohab curbed an imprecation as he tore his gaze away from Najeeb to look at Shehab. The man's black eyes were dancing with mischief, having evidently documented Mohab's reaction to Najeeb and Jala's reunion.

Another surge of savagery coursed in his blood. "Right now, I'm not sure that would be a bad thing."

Shehab chuckled, looking very pleased with Mohab's response. "If Najeeb drops dead, Jawad won't be far behind. He'd jump out of his fighter jet without a parachute if he found himself the crown prince of Saraya. Only Najeeb, in his endless wisdom and stamina, can deal with your uncle."

Mohab almost bared his teeth at Shehab. Hearing about Najeeb's endless wisdom—and stamina—was more fuel to his fire.

"And don't be too hard on Najeeb. It's only expected that any man would turn into a slobbering fool around Jala."

Mohab forced a smile to his taut face. "You trying to make me go rearrange my little cousin's face, and spend the rest of my engagement night in *your* little brother's dungeon?"

Shehab guffawed this time, definitely delighted with Mohab's vehemence, which he no doubt considered revealed the depth of his involvement with his sister. "Wouldn't *that* be a far more memorable engagement night than this inane dinner you and your fiancée imposed on us?"

Farah, Shehab's wife, turned to her husband, emerald eyes gleaming with curiosity. "What am I missing?"

Shehab scooped her to his side, his smile so bedeviling Mohab considered manually wiping it off his face. "Mohab here is so head over heels with Jala, he's having a male aggression crisis just watching her greet an old friend."

Farah waved her hand dismissingly. "Najeeb is a *really* old friend." Then she started recounting the story of Jala's and Najeeb's friendship.

Mohab suffered all he could before interjecting, "I already know all that. I was there the first time they met." When she looked confused, he explained further. "I was the one who led the extraction team and ended the hostage crisis."

Delight surged on Farah's face. "Oh, you're her knight in black-ops armor! How unbelievably romantic that after saving her life all these years ago, you'd reenter it as her prince charming!"

"That even tops the way we met, *ya rohi.*" Shehab gazed down at her with such indulgence, Mohab made a mental note to check his blood sugar as soon as he left their company.

Farah poked Shehab in equal adoration. "You mean when you set me up?" Mohab wanted to scoff "you, too?" as Farah turned to him with a mock-stern expression. "This perfect husband you see now first approached me swathed in Tuareg garb and masqueraded as someone else to seduce me into marrying him, thinking I was the former king of Zohayd's illegitimate daughter, all in the name of keeping Judar's peace."

Mohab couldn't hold back his scoff this time. It seemed seducing a woman for their kingdom's sake, then falling for her was an epidemic among the princes in this region.

"Let's get this engagement party under way, people," Kamal called out. "We're all experts at talking while eating."

As voices rose in approval and everyone moved back to the splendidly laid-out table, Mohab found himself surrounded by Jala's family while she was assimilated into his.

For the next hour a superb dinner was served, but he could taste none of it. Being separated from Jala and watching her with his cousins, with Najeeb, killed any appetite and any ability to enjoy her family's company.

At one point, as he stared at the grinning faces of the loving couples around the table, he reached a final conclusion. The Aal Masood family all suffered from toxic levels of happiness, and exposure to them was detrimental to his health. And sanity.

But he could see something besides sickening bliss on their faces. It was the shrewd realization that all was not as it should be with him and Jala. He waited with bated breath for someone to allude to this, but as if to stop their suspicion from becoming conviction, Jala left his cousins and came to stand behind Farooq.

Leaning over her oldest brother, she draped supple arms over his shoulders and kissed his cheek. "Can I have my fiancé back now? Cross-examined him to your heart's content?"

Her arm brushed against him and her hair swished forward, deluging him in her scent. Everything inside him clamored, almost drowning Farooq's guffaw.

"As if. You've got yourself one tight-lipped groom-to-be here. Figures, though, with what he does for a living. But the poor guy barely touched his dinner since he was busy eating you up. I don't think he even heard most of what we said to him."

Kamal chuckled. "I bet Mohab's ideal engagement dinner would have been having you alone somewhere secluded by the sea. I think we only managed to torture him with this dinner."

"Which is as it should be," Shehab said, winking at her. "In another age, we would have made him roam the desert in search of mythical treasures, then return to jump through hoops of fire for the privilege of your hand."

Mohab twisted his lips at her brothers. "Braving the desert unarmed and on foot, and then ending my trek by battling hungry hyenas over a fire pit *would* have been preferable to sitting across this ridiculously wide table from Jala throughout our so-called engagement party." He swept the three men a challenging look. "You *should* test me. The honor and privilege of her hand demands every proof that I actually deserve it. So prepare your trials. The more impossible, the better."

And he meant every word. He'd do anything for Jala. For this wasn't a matter of wanting to get her out of his system anymore. This was about winning her. Properly this time. And forever. He finally faced what he'd avoided acknowledging for years: what she was to him. This woman he'd wanted from the first moment, who he had pined for through the years of alienation, who he had watched over and learned from.

He'd never stopped loving her. And with everything she'd done and still did, every breath she took, she kept proving to him that he'd always been destined to love her.

He loved her now more than he ever had or even believed possible.

Feeling her eyes on him after his impassioned pledge,

he turned the force of his conviction on her, told her, word-lessly, but with everything in him, what he felt.

Meeting her eyes, he felt her spirit touch his, as it had from the very beginning. Now, even through the barrier she'd erected between them since that fateful night, it jolted through him again, how kindred it felt, how deep her hold over him was, how absolute. And he no longer wanted to sever it. He only wanted to cherish and revel in it. He only wanted to convince her to let him in again, to let him love her with everything he had, as he'd failed to in the past.

But something in her eyes sent his heart hammering. That vulnerability. And something else. Pain. Bottom-less pain.

It disturbed him so much it had him on his feet, just as Farooq stood to vacate his place for her.

Heart ramming his rib cage, he held her seat as she sat, trying to catch her gaze again, to confirm what he'd seen. But there was nothing but a bright, neutral smile as she murmured thanks and looked away as her brothers con-tinued poking and prodding him.

"No surprises here, Mission Impossible Man," Shehab said. "Wrestling impossible odds and facing lethal dan-gers must be easier for you than sitting still through a so-cial function."

Kamal sighed. "Wait till you're king. You'll suffer through those till you want to *cause* mayhem to escape them."

Taking Jala's place between his cousins, Farooq chimed in, "Hmm, I can make use of your willingness to do any-thing for Jala. I have some chronic…problems I need taken care of."

Reaching for the hand Jala rested on the table, he envel-oped it, a thrill going through him when she relinquished it to him. "Make me a list and consider them resolved."

Farooq grinned at Jala. "I'm sold. I like your fiancé. It's very handy to have a cleanup expert in the family."

"How about you ask him for a thousand red camels in the bargain?" Carmen ribbed her husband.

Everyone laughed at Carmen's allusion to one of the most famous folklore stories in the region, the immortal love story of Antarah and Ablah. Antarah, a slave who won his freedom through heroic feats, asked for his beloved's hand, only for her father to get rid of his nuisance by sending Antarah on an impossible mission to acquire rare camels from far-flung enemy territory, alone, unarmed and having nothing to bargain with. Antarah, of course, accomplished all this, and in the end won his Ablah.

If only everyone knew *his* mission impossible—winning back what he'd lost of Jala's heart and then reaching the parts he'd never been able to touch—was far harder than any overwhelming odds they could throw at him.

After an interval of gaiety as they exchanged anecdotes and tales from the past about more men in his situation, dessert was served.

Jawad, who'd been the most outspoken of his cousins during the evening, grinned at him so widely he wanted to hurl a plate between his perfect teeth. "When Najeeb told us Mohab was getting hitched, we just had to see the impossibility of who'd made him consider this suicidal move."

"Then we see Jala…and the rest of you ladies—" Haroon made a theatrical gesture around the table "—and now we know. Judar is the ultimate babe producer…and magnet."

Najeeb glared at his younger brothers. "I knew it was the biggest mistake I've made in recent memory letting you two tag along. Now I know how the enmity between our families started. It must have been instigated by men with big mouths and bigger eyes, like you."

"Chill, bro." Jawad grinned unrepentantly. "Those guys

know for a fact they have rare jewels that anyone with a heartbeat would admire." He flashed the ladies another killer smile. "I bet they'd be offended if we pretended we didn't notice."

"Yeah." Haroon smirked at Najeeb. "So maybe it was a tight ass like you, one who couldn't take a joke or wholesome admiration, who started the enmities."

Najeeb looked heavenward, then over at the Aal Masoods, focusing on Kamal. "See what I have to put up with? Now that you've seen my spare heirs, I hope you really appreciate yours."

"Oh, our baby brother, Kamal, appreciates the hell out of us." Farooq chuckled, eliciting an exasperated growl from Kamal. "You on the other hand, Najeeb, are to be pitied…"

Having had enough and still holding Jala's hand, Mohab rose. "And here I want to thank you all for celebrating this momentous occasion with me and Jala." He panned his gaze among Jala's family. "But though I truly appreciate the welcome you've shown me, and *forood walaa'ee wa ta'ahtee,* my pledge of allegiance and obedience stands. Kamal was right. There's nothing I want more than to have Jala to myself, at least for part of the evening, to make its memory a perfect one. So please, continue to celebrate, and excuse us as we go have our own personal celebration."

As he pulled back the chair for Jala and she stood up lithely, his heart again convulsed when he noticed the glance she exchanged with Najeeb. Shehab and Farooq ribbed him some more, while Kamal said nothing, the gaze encompassing him and Jala still…unconvinced.

Kamal must realize Jala's lack of interaction with him wasn't a matter of shyness in front of her brothers, or on account of the suddenness of their resumed relationship and its rapid development. After all, Kamal was a man versed in both his sister's nature and in matters of the heart. He must realize something was wrong.

But still giving him all the support he could, Kamal waved his hand in mock imperiousness. "You may be excused, but only because we now have said pledge of allegiance and obedience, and can do anything at all with you."

As everyone laughed again, Jala said, "It's only fair to warn you that while you'll have the allegiance, you'll be out of luck where the obedience is concerned. From personal experience you know where *that* will be expended." She turned and winked at her sisters-in-law. "Right, ladies?"

As her family all laughed, and Jawad and Haroon begged to hear some obedience examples—to fortify their resolve *never* to marry—she waved a final goodbye. Then she turned and headed out of the dining room, with him a step behind her.

Once they were away from the royal quarters, he opened the first door he found and pulled her into the chamber's darkness, lifting her off the ground, already kissing her.

Her gasp filled him as her lips opened beneath his. Tasting the tart sweetness of berry sauce on her tongue, he groaned, plunging deeper, seeking more of her taste, demanding her surrender. For long minutes, she gave it to him as he pressed her against the door, opening her thighs around his hips and grinding at her core through their clothes, simulating the possession he was going insane for.

"Jala, *habibati...*"

She suddenly lurched and pushed at him.

Putting her back on her feet, he twisted a hand in the luxury of her hair, able to see her now that his sight had adapted to the faint lights coming from the windows. "Let me love you, *ya jalati.* Stop pushing me away. Let me close again. I know you want me as much as I want you."

Her breasts still heaved against his chest, her body

arched involuntarily into his even when her words rejected him. "I don't care what I want. This isn't what I agreed to."

"Then agree to this now. To giving us another chance."

"*No*. I don't want another chance. I want to play my part until we're sure your uncle will sign the treaties, then I want to leave. This is what I want to do. What I *need* to do."

The desperation in her voice struck him in his vitals, made him stagger away.

And because he had admitted to himself that he loved her, only wanted her to be happy whatever the cost to him, he couldn't pursue his seduction anymore. Not if, for some reason he couldn't fathom, it distressed her that much. It might kill him to let her go, but he'd rather die than hurt her.

His shoulders slumped with defeat. "My uncle is sending you a set from the royal treasury. It's his way of saying the peace treaty is as good as signed."

After a long moment of staring at him, she whispered, "That's great. I mean, that you think he'd sign, not about the jewels."

He waved her qualification away. He knew she cared nothing about material things, and not because she had plenty of them. She made no use of her status in any way, not for herself. She used all her privileges to serve the world.

"I have the drafts of the treaties ready, and after Kamal approves them, I'll present my uncle with them. My package for Saraya is very generous, but as you believe, he wouldn't have felt secure enough or irreversibly connected to Judar without a union of blood. Which he now believes he'll have, thanks to your cooperation. I don't expect he'll pose any further threat to peace."

Her eyes wavered. This had clearly come out of left field for her. She'd expected him to continue his pursuit, his seduction. And here he was telling her there was no longer any reason for her to play along at all.

He exhaled roughly. "I had my chance with you, and I blew it. Or maybe there was never a chance to be had with you, then or now. I will take part in all the wedding preparations, so both my uncle and Kamal believe everything is in order and on schedule. I'll push for an early signing of the treaties, which, now that my uncle is so amenable, I expect will be soon. Once he signs, I'll reveal the truth and absorb whatever fallout ensues, away from you. Until then, I'll give Kamal some convincing reason for leaving the palace. I'll go in the morning, so you don't have to put up with seeing me again."

Nine

Something tore Mohab from the tentacles of fitful sleep.

The heart that no exertion or danger managed to send thundering, thundered now, past the comfort zone and into distress.

It only ever beat that way for Jala.

Jala. Had something happened to…?

He shot up in bed, alarm swamping him.

"Sorry I startled you."

Mohab felt as if he'd been hit by lightning.

Jala. Here. On his bed.

Leaning across him, body draped in white silk, silvered by the moon's cool illumination, hair raining in sheets of solid darkness across the thighs twisted in his sheets, she looked like a night goddess, his every fantasy made flesh.

This had been the dream he'd been having. That she'd come to him. He'd felt her entering his room and…

He was still asleep!

But he felt awake. She felt real. But she couldn't be real. She'd said no. Such an impassioned, desperate no.

So had he gone over the deep end? He'd been building up to a breakdown for years now. Was this it? He'd start wish-fulfilling wide-awake? Having delusions?

"I couldn't stay away anymore. I couldn't let you leave without telling you I still want you. Now more than ever."

He *was* hearing those words. She was saying them. He knew because even he couldn't imagine the way she made them sound, wouldn't be that ambitious, that delusional as to make them such a throb of passion, such a scald of longing.

She was here. And she had said those words. Not the ones he needed, but still far more than he deserved.

I still want you. Now more than ever.

On their thousandth rotation inside of a single second, he reached out a hand to her face, still half expecting to find nothing but emptiness, for her image to dissipate.

His fingers touched the hot velvet of her cheek.

Groaning at the confirmation, he swung around to his bedside lamp. He had to see her better than the crescent moon through his open windows allowed.

With the chamber flooded in golden light, he turned to her and saw that the lace and satin nightgown and matching robe were cream, not white, the color offsetting the rich gold of her polished flesh.

Then he saw her eyes. Unlocked for him at last, letting him see inside her, see the full measure of her hunger.

Already hard beyond pain, heart trembling with disbelief still, he reached back to her, careful not to make any sudden moves, still afraid this dream might come to an end as every tortured one had in the past six years.

When he was an inch from touching her again, she did something that stopped his heart. What she'd done that night he'd first taken her to his penthouse.

She melted back on the bed, as if she couldn't support herself anymore, threw her arms above her head, arched in surrender, a sultry moan spilling from deep rose lips.

"I *want* you, Mohab."

Surging with her demand, he came over her, straddled her hips, cupping her face in trembling hands. "*Aih,* want me, *ya habibati, atawassal elaiki*—I beg you. I'm yours to want."

"Mohab...kiss my lips, give me yours..."

She reached up and grabbed his hair. This was why he'd let it grow, because she'd once told him she wanted it longer to pull him by, to tether him closer to her on their wild rides. Now she dragged his head with it, surging up to crash her mouth against his. Her tongue delved inside him, tangling in abandon with his.

He let her storm him, let her show him the measure of her pent-up craving and impatience. Then he took over.

He'd show her six years' worth of hunger. Then he'd give her satiation well worth the wait.

He bit into her lower lip, showing her the power of his own craving, before he suckled it inside his mouth in long, smooth pulls, drawing more plumpness into her succulent flesh, then plunging his tongue inside her.

Her whimpers became incessant, her hands clenched in his hair as she wrestled with him for deeper surrender, the pain of her urgency excruciating pleasure. She crushed her breasts into his chest, cushioning him, one leg escaping his prison to wind around his hip in abandon. She was showing him she wanted anything he'd do to her. Anything at all.

Then she moaned into his mouth, "Touch me, Mohab, all over. Do everything to me, don't be gentle...I can't bear for you to be gentle.... I want your full force. I want you inside me, hard and long and now...*now,* Mohab. I can't wait anymore...I can't wait...."

Elation sizzled in his blood. She'd never been this vocal, never told him what she wanted or how she wanted it.

"*Aih, gulili aish betridi*—tell me what you want, *ya galbi.*" His voice shook as he pushed the robe off her shoulders, then raised her arms over her head once more and, in a luxurious upward sweep, freed her from her nightgown. She only had bikini panties beneath, which he took off, as well. Then he pulled back to fill his eyes with her. *"Ma ajmalek, ya habibati, ajmal men zekrayati, men ahlami."*

"*You* are." She pressed kisses onto any part of him she reached, his chest, arms, hands. "So much more beautiful than my memories and my dreams."

Arousal hammering in his blood, pounding in his loins, he sculpted her in a frenzy of memory and rediscovery, owned each remembered inch of her silken skin, kneading new curves, digging into strength and soft femininity. Her flesh hummed beneath his fingers, electrifying him.

Her teeth sank into his hand. "Touch my breasts...."

A chuckle revved in his chest, resonating his delight that she was so aggressively demanding his pleasuring. He loved it.

"*Amrek ya hayati,* command me." He took their weight in his palms and stared at their ripened perfection, stroking their turgid flesh in wonder, squeezing their incredible resilience, circling the buds he'd tasted during so many rides to ecstasy. They were thicker now, darker, more mouthwatering.

With a long whimper, she attacked his pajama bottoms. He let her push them down his hips, growling as she released an erection that had long hardened to steel. Rising to release himself fully, he watched her fling herself up at him, then rumbled as she bunched her hands in his back muscles and latched her teeth into the muscles of his abdomen and torso, writhing against him as if she'd mingle their flesh.

He subdued her back to the bed and she wound herself around him, her voice a thread about to snap. "Come inside me, Mohab...don't make me wait anymore...please... *please*..."

He devoured her pleas, unleashed now that he knew only the savagery of his need would satisfy her.

His lips relinquishing hers, he sowed a path of kisses and suckles lower, until he possessed her breasts, raining bites over their engorged beauty until she crushed his head to her, mashing her flesh into his mouth. He latched on to one nipple, then the other, alternating heavy pulls and sharp nips, each rewarded by a lurch and a shriek.

When he felt her stimulation becoming distress, his hands dragged over her soft, satiny flesh to her core. Spreading her, he slid between her feminine lips, growling with the extent of her readiness. He was coming apart needing to be inside her, but he had to prepare her. For he *wouldn't* be gentle when he took her. As she'd commanded. Clamping his lips on hers, he probed her, plunged two, then three fingers inside her hot channel.

Her thighs clamped his hand, her fingers dug into his scalp as her body convulsed, sharp, spasmodic squeals gusting into his lungs. She was climaxing. With but a touch. He'd aroused her that much.

He allowed himself a moment to watch her in the throes of satisfaction, the sight he'd starved for for six bleak years. Then he took her mouth again, doing to it what his fingers still did to her core, feeding her frenzy, loving every jerk, drinking every last whimper until she slumped in his arms, all precious, satisfied woman.

Or so he thought. In a minute, her lips found his chest again, her leg rubbing against his hardness. Imprisoning it in both of his, he clamped the hand that greedily caressed his shaft.

"I want to touch you, Mohab, taste you...."

The memory alone of her head bowed at his loins, her hair spread on his thighs, the sweep of her back, the flare of her hips as she rubbed herself against his legs like a feline in heat, moaning her pleasure as she worshipped him with trembling hands and swollen lips, almost made him come.

"Later, Jala. Own me later. *Areed aklek, akhullusek*—I want to devour you, finish you."

"No...just come inside me...." She wrapped her legs around his hips, ground her moist heat over his erection.

He savored the torture for a moment, absorbing her need, then opened her folds with the head of his erection, and she mewled and spread herself wider for him, the sound and sight almost making his skull burst. He circled the engorged bud of her arousal, drawing more keens, more prodding twists in his hair. Then he slid from her grasp and moved between her thighs.

Before she could protest again, he took her feminine lips in a voracious kiss, his tongue lapping her in long sweeps. Her protests fractured only when he suckled her bud until he had her thrashing, begging. When he knew she couldn't stand anymore, he bit down on her.

The force of her release razed through his body, almost triggering his. He again pushed three fingers inside her, sharpening her pleasure, lapping up its flood until her voice broke and her body slumped.

Still lapping at her, soothing now, he rested his head over her trembling thigh, tenderness a rising tide through the sustained agony. How he'd missed pleasuring her.

Her shaking hands wound in his hair again, dragging him up by it as he'd dreamed she'd do for so long. He obeyed her, swept up over her, sank languorously into her kiss. Reveling in her hands roaming his body, he could feel her extracting his soul, reclaiming him with her raging need.

She suckled his earlobe, bit it, sending a million arrows lodging into his erection, whispered in a voice roughened by abandon and satisfaction, "*Now* will you come inside me?"

"*Enti to'morini*...you only have to command me."

"I did nothing but command you...to no avail."

A guffaw ripped out of him. The fact that she was teasing him now was so unexpected, so delightful.

His hands dug into the buttocks undulating against him. "You call this 'no avail'?"

In answer, she pressed her body and lips to his. "I call anything that doesn't end with you inside me that."

"I spent six years planning all the ways I'd pleasure you when I finally got my hands and lips on you again, *ya rohi*."

She pulled him back over her, eyes feverish. "I only want one way. You. Inside me. *Now,* Mohab."

His heart boomed with gratitude and pride. She didn't want just any pleasure, no matter how fierce. She wanted the pleasure of union, with him.

It was humbling that she desired him as much as before and more. But his passion had intensified through the forging of denial and disappointment, frustration and separation, though mostly by total, unconditional love. Why had hers strengthened? He couldn't tell, could only give thanks.

For one last moment before he joined them, he held her eyes as he loomed over her, and they swallowed him whole.

"Take me."

Obeying her desperate demand, he thrust into her in one savage plunge, sheathing himself inside her tight heat to the hilt, hurtling home, his only home. Her scream felt as if it tore from her lungs, pure, excruciating pleasure, as his bellow had been. She arched up in a steep bow, seeking his possession, needing his urgency and ferocity, and he gave it to her. He withdrew all the way, then forged back even deeper, harder, the near impossible fit driving him out of his mind, until he'd built to a jackhammering rhythm with his full force behind it.

Too soon, her screams merged as she bucked beneath him…then shattered in convulsions that clamped her around him, wrenching at his length in a fit of release. He rode the breakers of her orgasm, withdrawing and plunging in a fury, feeding her frenzy until her screeches stifled and her heart accelerated beyond the danger zone, her tears pouring thickly.

"Come with me…."

Her sob broke him. He let go, buried himself to her womb, wished he could bury all of himself inside her, and surrendered to the most ferocious orgasm he'd ever known, jetting his essence into her depths in gush after agonizing gush, roaring his love, his worship.

"Ahebbek ya hayati, ya rohi…Jala, aabodek…"

Pleasure stormed through him, held him in a merciless vice for long minutes, then it suddenly unleashed its grip, let him breathe, unlocked his muscles. He collapsed over her, driving deeper into their merging.

When he had control over his body again, he withdrew to look down at her, and his heart swelled at the sight of the goddess she'd become. A soundly slumbering one right now. His lips shook on a smile of satisfaction. So he could still pleasure her into oblivion.

Gratitude swamped him again as he made his pledge to the fates. If he couldn't have her love, he'd wallow in her desire, fulfill her every need, lavish all his love and trust and honor on her. He'd keep her hungrier for more still, do anything to keep her beside him.

Until he made her love him. For real. And forever.

Jala jerked out of a place of total darkness and bliss to the sight of Mohab over her, the feel of him inside her.

His weight felt like the gravity holding her universe together. The universe that had spun out of control when he'd told her he'd leave and she wouldn't be seeing him again.

The eruption of despair had overwhelmed her. She'd pushed him away, thinking she'd been defending herself, saving her sanity. But the idea of losing him again and forever had torn aside inhibitions, rationality, even survival. She'd had to have him again, even if the cost was eternal misery. Nothing had changed, or would ever change. She would always need him beyond self-preservation. And she'd thrown herself into the heaven and hell of his arms again.

The conflagration that had followed, what he'd done to her, proved she'd only forgotten how it had felt to be with him. Or that this ecstasy was new.

It *was* new. And far more potentially destructive for it.

"Jala, *habibati*..." Mohab's voice cascaded like warm midnight waters over her as he turned them around, draping her over him, maintaining their union. "Are you all right?"

No. You exist and I'll never be all right.

Forcing herself to keep it light, she rubbed her face into his pectorals, response gushing again in the core he occupied as the glistening sprinkle of his chest hair tickled her lips. "You really need to ask?"

He smoothed large, calloused hands over her back. "You were moaning. I thought I was too heavy so I took most of my weight off you, changed positions, but you're still tense. You're uncomfortable with me inside you?"

He *was* too big, too thick, and it seemed as if he hadn't subsided at all. He did stretch her into an edge of pain that was addictive, overwhelming, and as he'd driven all that power inside her, it had been beyond exhilarating. The idea of all that he was, focused in one act of sheer desperation, as much at her mercy as she was at his, filled her, body and soul. She'd thought her younger self had experienced the height of shattering emotions, and that was why she'd felt so empty and bereft when she'd lost him. Turned out, she'd known nothing.

When her answer was delayed, he started raising her off him. She panicked, squeezed him with all her strength, kept him inside her.

He threw his head back on a bass groan, his mane fanning on the rumpled sheets, his hands digging into her buttocks, thrusting his own buttocks up to grind himself farther inside her.

She collapsed on him, a cry of shocked pleasure opening her lips on his corded neck as he nudged her womb. *"Mohab..."*

Rising to a sitting position with her straddling his hips, he leaned against the headboard, held her hips in his palms and raised her until the head of his erection emerged from her entrance, then he let her sink over the girth slicked in their pleasure.

"Ride me, *ya rohi*. Take me and take your pleasure of me."

Feeling faint with sensation, she braced herself against the worked wood, thighs trembling as she tried to scale his length. She'd managed only half when his mouth engulfed one nipple, his fingers twisting the other.

She crashed down on him, felt him push into her cervix. *"Mohab...please..."*

He took her arms from their slump, placed them on his shoulders, then held her hips and moved her up and down, traveling the length of his erection in leisurely journeys to the rhythm of his long, deep suckles of her nipples until the pressure in her core threatened to implode. "Before you, I never dreamed pleasure like that existed. I never want to stop pleasuring you, *ya hayat galbi*."

Life of my heart. One of the extravagant endearments that he'd lavished on her in the past.

Hearing it now nearly tipped her over into the abyss, made her wail, "Mohab…I can't… Too much…"

Again he understood. Easing her onto her back, he rose above her, spreading her wider around his bulk as he lunged forward, letting her feel the rawness of the strength that could and had pulverized men twice her size, now leashed to become carnality and cherishing instead. He stretched her around his invasion and stilled, throbbing in her depths, his fiery eyes holding her streaming ones, until she was one exposed nerve ending.

"*You* are too much. Everything you are. Take me, Jala, all of me." He withdrew as he talked, then rammed back into her.

As if this was his first thrust all over again, she shredded her larynx on a shriek. She dug her fingernails into his buttocks, wanting him to stab her to the heart, destroy her once and for all.

And he did.

She convulsed, stilled into a whiteout before everything detonated, wave after wave radiating from his driving manhood to raze her, reform her for the next sweep.

Then it shot beyond her ability to withstand. He'd joined her in this darkest ecstasy, roaring his completion, his orgasm boosting hers as surge after surge of his seed splashed into her womb, finishing her with delight…and desolation.

From the depths of satiation, Jala opened eyes that felt glued shut. Her breath hitched, and her body heated instantaneously as she found herself enveloped in him.

Mohab. As in all her dreams, as in those five months they'd been lovers. Curved around her, his legs encompassing her, his head propped on one hand, the other sweeping her in caresses, his eyes and lips radiating pure male satisfaction.

She reached out, ran numb fingertips down his beard. It was amazingly soft, just the right length to lose any stubbly feel. Just remembering how it had felt against her lips, against every inch of her, was enough to have her squirming with arousal again. Not to mention the feel of his hair as she'd binged on the freedom of twisting her hands in it and pulling on it.

"How long have I been out?" Her voice was thick and raspy. The voice of a woman who'd been savagely pleasured. She did feel gloriously sore, every cell shrieking with life.

"An hour or so," he teased. "Watching you tumble into unconsciousness in the aftermath of my possession, then documenting your abandon to slumber, every inch flushed and drained with satiation…" He sighed deeply, rubbed his beard against her shoulder as he plastered her more securely to his length. "It remains the most fantastic sight I've ever seen. It *is* the most gratifying thing in the world, knowing that I can still knock you out with pleasure."

"Anything I can do for your male ego," she croaked.

He hugged her exuberantly before pulling back, his eyes turning serious. "Mine is all tied up in my ability to satisfy you, Jala. And now that I know for certain that this is something only I can do, I won't let you fight our need anymore. We must and will be together."

She closed her eyes, warding off the intensity in his.

It did nothing to reduce the brutality of temptation. She couldn't resist him or her need for him. But she had to lay down limits before he swallowed her whole.

She opened her eyes. "As I just proved, I want you beyond my ability to resist. So I will be with you."

He sat up, his eyes intent. "What do you mean...with me?"

"I'll marry you. For those six months you proposed."

Ten

It had been a torturous whirlwind since that night she'd surrendered to her need for Mohab and told him she'd take his original offer of a six-month marriage.

When she had, he'd brooded down at her for a long moment…then he'd proceeded to plunder her throughout the rest of the night…and morning.

That had been three weeks ago. Time had never passed so slowly. Or so fast.

And tonight was their wedding night.

Once Mohab had secured her agreement, he'd pushed for cutting short the intended three-month engagement. Now he knew he'd have a sure response from his uncle after their wedding, he wanted it as soon as possible. Especially since it was clear, after their one night together, that they'd have no more until they were officially married.

After their explosive reunion, they'd suddenly found themselves surrounded at all times. She suspected Kamal's eyes in the palace had reported her nocturnal visit to

Mohab, and to curtail the scandal that would surely ensue if it became known the princess of Judar was entering her intended's bed prematurely, he'd conspired to keep them apart. Since Kamal *had* alluded to the fact that the anticipation before the ceremony invariably made the wedding night all the more...special, she was positive that her constant state of deprivation was her dastardly brother's doing.

But maybe she shouldn't be so impatient to start the marriage that would have her in Mohab's bed again. Because once it did start, she'd start counting down the minutes to its end.

But knowing there would be nothing permanent between them, she'd already decided to take what she could of him, with him, hoard memories for the future. A future she'd always known would be empty, but would now be bleak.

Emptying a chest tight with futility, she forced burning eyes to take in the vista from her window. She wouldn't let heartache dissolve into tears and face tonight with eyes that told its story. She had to play her part tonight, had to honor Mohab in front of his people, fill her temporary position as his bride and queen as best she could.

But even the land that felt untouched by time, being exposed to its ambiance of purity and the serenity that permeated it, failed to imbue her with any measure of calm.

Though this land had touched her on her most fundamental level from the moment she'd laid eyes on it, just like its most influential son had, she still regretted that she'd agreed when Mohab had insisted their wedding take place here.

Jareer. His ancestral land. Where he would become king tonight. And she'd become his queen. Temporarily.

Once she'd lost the right to be here, the memory of experiencing this place with him would be one more injury and loss to live with.

At Mohab's insistence, Kamal had relinquished the right to have his sister's wedding in Judar. He'd thoroughly approved of Mohab wanting to make her his—and Jareer's—queen on the same night of his *joloos,* when he claimed the newly forged throne.

Since being this accommodating was so unlike Kamal, she'd teasingly accused him of letting Mohab walk all over him just so he'd end her long-lamented spinsterhood. Kamal had only teased back, "Of course, why else?"

And here she was, in Zahara, what passed for Jareer's capital.

They'd come two weeks ago to prepare for the dual celebration. By *they,* she meant *everyone.* Her getting hitched was such a big deal that her family had left Judar unattended to make sure her wedding went, well, without a hitch.

Not that Mohab was letting anyone do anything. Apart from Carmen, who was a master event planner, and Aliyah, a world-renowned artist who had eagerly taken charge of dressing everyone, he had adamantly refused to let anyone lift a finger in anything but recreation. As such, he spent his every waking hour being the perfect host to everyone.

While acting as their tour guide, he'd been a mine of information. According to him, this area had been settled since prehistoric times, and to prove it he'd taken them to see the local caves with their ancient rock paintings. He'd showed them the monuments of every culture that had left their mark on the region, with the most influential being Ottoman, Persian and Indian, but all wrapped up in an Arabian feel.

Apart from the many tourist spots the region boasted, it had surprised her how much there was to do around here. There was a vast array of outdoor activities—from hiking to dune skating to horseback riding, to swimming in and lazing around sparkling springs, to bonfire banquets at night.

It had been bittersweet watching Mohab dote on her sisters-in-law and nephews and nieces and bond with her brothers. They had all taken to him—especially Kamal—which caused her extra delight...and dejection, when she knew that this would all end on a prearranged date.

As it had to.

But through it all, she'd done everything she could not to dwell on that inevitable end before they even began. And in those moments that she managed to forget, she'd reveled in his spoiling. For *how* he'd spoiled her.

Though nothing he did could make up for being unable to have him again. Since they'd come here, he hadn't even had a chance to kiss her. Well, he did, constantly, but only her hands, shoulders and cheeks. And then there were the scorching caresses, the devouring, brooding glances, the laden-with-promise smiles and the lavish words of praise. Everything had kept her on the verge of spontaneous combustion.

Sighing, she focused on the scene in the distance, with Zahara's houses arranged in graduated compositions of whitewashed adobe and red and yellow-ocher stone. At night, before the full moon rose, they were only shades of gray, but in the daylight they looked like an explosion of flowers atop the sandstone hills.

Mohab had insisted on coming here by land, saying the scenery on the way was worth the six-hour drive from Durgham. And it had been. She'd never seen such variations to the desert, the terrain flowing from undulating dunes to hilly pastures to mountainous heights to combinations of everything.

Then this castle had materialized in the horizon, reigning over Zahara, and it had taken her breath away.

Nestled in the containment of the craggy mountain

that overlooked the vista of Zahara, against an ocean of dunes, it crouched behind soaring ancient walls shielded by battlements that summoned to mind Saladin and the Crusades. That night it had loomed against an impossibly starry night, with torchlight fluctuating from the inside and the guard posts shedding their firelight on the outside, drenching it in a deeper, supernatural tinge.

It had been the Aal Kussaimis' stronghold until the time of Sheikh Numair, Mohab's maternal great-grandfather. But after Jareer had signed the treaty with Saraya, and no one inhabited it anymore, this place had fallen into decay.

But Mohab had had it restored in order to boost Jareer's tourist business. He'd succeeded, since the citadel had become one of the region's most frequented historical sites. Like her, tourists found it a once-in-a-lifetime experience, as they wandered through its maze of passages, extensive grounds and interconnected structures, feeling as if they were taking a stroll in the past. Tonight the place would rise against a full moon, and be bathed in the lights of the extensive tent set just outside its walls for the wedding celebration.

She'd expected the guests to include world movers and shakers, but to hear that two presidents and one king from the Western world were attending had made her feel the gravity of the whole situation. This wasn't just a royal wedding, but a major political event. Mohab was claiming more than a bride tonight—he was claiming the throne of a land that would feature heavily in global power from now on.

Standing up, she looked around the chamber Mohab had assigned her till their wedding. He'd restored every inch to its original condition with painstaking authenticity, but had outfitted it with every modern luxury and amenity. She could see herself living here, going away only for work, but always coming back home here.

Home. She'd never felt she had a home. But this majestic place—which was permeated with Mohab's unique, indomitable essence—felt like home.

Not that it mattered how it felt. Her stay here was only a transient one. Now, even the hour she'd managed to negotiate alone before everyone swarmed around her to prepare her for the most momentous night of her life was almost up.

"You hour is up, sweetie."

Groaning, she turned to her sisters-in-law, who were striding through the chamber's ancient oak door. "You must have a stopwatch in your lineage, Aliyah."

The ladies laughed at her lament as Aliyah ushered in her ladies-in-waiting with everything Jala would be wearing. Jala's only input had been picking a color scheme. Living in jeans or utilitarian dresses, she hadn't been about to trust herself with an opinion beyond that. Needing to look the part of Mohab's bride and queen, she'd left it all to Aliyah's artistry and experience as a queen, and to the other two ladies who were far better versed than she was in fulfilling the demands of their titles.

Carmen clapped impatiently. "Hop to it! Your hour of meditation crunched the time to get you ready to a measly thirty minutes!"

Jala bowed. "Yes, O Mistress of Magnificent Events."

Farah chuckled as she fanned her hands in excitement. "You don't know the half of it. Everything you think you saw, or thought the preparations would amount to, is *nothing* to the end result. And I thought Carmen made *my* wedding rival a fable from *One Thousand and One Nights!*"

Carmen chuckled. "I actually didn't do much this time. Your Mohab is so ultraefficient, not to mention head over heels in love with you, he's the one who's done most of the work to give you the best wedding in modern times."

Jala was an old hand by now in maintaining a bright smile when everyone kept stating how much Mohab was in love with her. They had no idea how it actually was between them. But how could they? To them, it must seem like a fairy tale, and they must believe that everything Mohab lavished on her was based on what they all defined as love. None of them could imagine that her relationship was nothing like theirs, that his involvement was fueled by pure passion and garnished by convenience, and that the whole thing had an expiration date.

Putting down a jewelry box with Saraya's royal insignia that contained the heirloom pieces King Hassan had bestowed on Jala, insisting she wear them for her wedding, Carmen grinned. "And this magnificent place worked on its own. Any touch I put was multiplied tenfold by its magic."

Jala could well believe it. Not that this diminished Carmen's and Mohab's efforts in any way.

Farah nodded. "And the people of Jareer themselves. I've never seen a collective so ready for entertainment and versed in preparing celebrations."

"Yeah, and I thought the people in Judar were like that in comparison to the States," Carmen said. "But being here showed me how modern life had taken root in Judar, too, preoccupying everyone. Here every birth and wedding, cultural or religious occasion is a feast *everyone* attends and takes part in."

Farah grinned her pleasure. "And we've been the lucky recipients of their enthusiasm and expertise through our stay. It's going to be such a downer going back to indoor court life and our relatively isolated family lives now." She winked. "Good thing we have our men to keep us… intensely entertained."

Chuckling in corroboration, Aliyah appeared from behind the screen that doubled as the dressing room. "We're ready for you, Jala. As Carmen said, hop to it."

Jala did hop to it. She wanted this over with.

In under ten minutes, she was looking at herself in

amazement in the full-length gilded mirror. It was a good thing she'd left herself in Aliyah's hands. That image reflected at her *was* a princess. And a future queen.

Still not believing how the parts she'd had fitted on her had come together, she ran her hands down the incredible deep gold Persian/Indian creation that accentuated her curves and offset her coloring. It had a deep off-shoulder décolletage, a nipped waistline and a layered skirt with a tapering trail. It was heavily embellished in breathtakingly intricate floral designs of silver and bronze thread and was worked with sequins, beads, pearls, crystals and appliqué in every shade of burnt orange, crimson and garnet. The *lehenga*-like skirt was organza over silk taffeta, embroidery sweeping down its lines in arcs. Everything was topped off by a lace and chiffon *dupatta* veil, perched on her swept-up hair, in gradations of gold and crimson with scalloped, heavily embellished edges.

She stood gazing at herself as the ladies adorned her in the priceless pieces of Sarayan treasure, which they thought were part of her *shabkah,* but in reality would only be on loan. The centerpiece of the collection was a twenty-four-karat gold necklace that spread over her collarbones and cascaded to fill most of the generous décolletage tapering just above her barely visible cleavage. It was the most amazing and delicate lacy pattern she'd ever seen in a piece of jewelry, inlaid with diamonds and citrines, with a gigantic bloodred ruby in the center of the design.

The other pieces matched the necklace's delicacy and intricacy, from the shoulder-length earrings to the *tikka* headpiece, to the armband, web ring and anklet. By the time she was adorned in everything, she looked like a walking exhibition, but had to admit—she looked *fantastic.* If no one noticed the shadows in her eyes, that was.

But even those were obscured by the makeup Aliyah

applied. When Aliyah stood back and said, "Voila!" Jala could barely recognize herself.

"*Ya Ullah,* Aliyah," she groaned as she stood up. "Mohab will probably ask you what happened to his intended bride!"

Laughter rang around the chamber as Aliyah revolved around her one last time to ensure everything was in order. "You're just not used to putting any makeup on. You look exactly as you always do, but with a little emphasis."

"A little? I look like a makeup ad!"

"We women need something extra to face cameras, not like those men of ours who look fantastic in any conditions. But since you're the most beautiful woman ever, all you needed was a brush of mascara, a line of kohl and a smear of lipstick."

"The most beautiful woman ever, my foot!" Jala snorted.

Aliyah chuckled. "Being Kamal's female edition makes you incontestably that to me. But then Mohab thinks so, too, and certainly not because you look like Kamal."

"Are you ladies done making me and Mohab choke?"

Kamal. He was here to take her to her groom. And he was teasing them with the common belief that people choked when others talked about them.

He approached her, his eyes so loving, so proud, she was the one who choked and threw herself into his arms.

He hugged her off the ground, kissing her forehead. "My little, beloved sister—I am so happy you finally have someone to love you as you should be loved."

There was no stopping the tears from gushing this time. All she wanted to do was burrow into his powerful, protective arms and sob her heartache to him. If only...

Aliyah pounced to separate them before Jala smothered her face in Kamal's chest and spoiled all her efforts. "Postpone tear-inducing declarations to *el sabaheyah,* will you?"

Stepping away from Kamal, she feigned a smile. "If

you think you'll ambush me and Mohab tomorrow morning, pretending to congratulate us but really checking on the satisfactoriness of the consummation, you have another think coming."

"I don't care how old you are," Kamal growled. "Or that you're getting married. You're my baby sister and I'd rather not hear about you and consummation in the same sentence."

She poked him teasingly. "So you're okay with knowing it's happening, just don't want to *hear* about it?"

Kamal shuddered. "One more word and I take you back to Judar and put you where no man can get his paws on you."

Aliyah hooted. "My husband, the hopelessly overprotective brother."

Jala smirked. "Hope he's not as hopelessly old-fashioned a lover."

Kamal mock growled and lunged at her.

Everyone continued to laugh as they left her chambers and proceeded to where both the wedding and *joloos* rituals were taking place, picking up her bridal procession on the way. Jala was relieved no one had thought her overwrought moments had been anything more than the prewedding jitters of a woman about to enter into a union that would change her life forever.

As it would. Just not the way everyone thought it would.

Then everything stalled in her mind as she entered the massive hall in the heart of the citadel. Farah had been right. She'd seen the preparations, but couldn't have imagined how it would all come together.

Wrapped in the mist of musky incense, under the firelight of a thousand torches perched high on the stone walls in polished brass holders, the whole scene was a plunge into the most lavish eras of bygone empires, or even *One Thousand and One Nights*.

As her dazed glance swept the space, the details were almost too much to take in. Cascading satin banners with Jareer's tribal insignias. Acres of tulle and voile wrapping around columns, raining from the hundred-foot-high ceiling and spanning the elaborate Arabesque framework. And the hall that Mohab had installed exploding with flower arrangements. The hundreds of people present looked like sparkling gems themselves in all kinds of finery, from lavish modern evening gowns and tuxedos, to costumes that belonged in a masquerade.

Then everything ceased to exist. In the depths of the hall, on top of a maroon-satin covered platform, with two elaborately carved and gilded ceremonial chairs at his back, there he stood. Mohab.

His hair is loose. It was the first thing that burst into her mind. He'd never worn it down in public before. But now it brushed the top of his massive shoulders, its thick luxury and vitality gleaming with sun strands in the firelight.

The second thing that impinged on her hazy awareness was that he was dressed like he *had* stepped out of the Arabian Nights. Like everyone in her bridal procession, his clothes had the same color scheme, if in much darker tones. A burgundy *abaya* cascaded from his shoulders to his feet over a gold-beige top embroidered in his tribal motifs. Dark maroon pants clung to his muscled thighs before disappearing into darker leather boots.

He looked like the embodiment of the might of the desert, the implacability of the fates. And he glowed. She swore he did. From the inside. With power and distinction. And she loved him with everything in her. Despite the harsh lessons of the past and the permanent injuries lying in the future.

An eruption of thuds made her lurch, even though she'd known it was coming. The matrons of the tribe began her bridal procession with a boisterous percussive *zaffah* that was a variation of what she was used to in Judar.

She snatched a look behind her at the older women with their chins and temples tattooed. One of them was two feet to her side, whacking away at a *mihbaj* wooden grinder.

Then others joined on all the local percussive instruments—the tambourine-like *reg,* the bigger jangle-free *duff* and the vase-shaped hand drum called a *darabukkah.* After that rousing introduction, melody players joined in, an evocative droning emanating from the string *rababah,* and the squealing of reedlike *mizmar.* Then voices rose, from all around, singing congratulations to the bridegroom for his incomparable bride.

She found herself rushing beside Kamal, powered by Mohab's hunger that demanded her at his side. Once they were on top of the platform, her eyes clung to her most beloved people, Kamal and Mohab, locked in a firm embrace that exchanged pledge and trust, before withdrawing to grip each other by one hand, while their other exchanged her from brother to husband.

Then she was clasped tight to Mohab's side, drowning in him, in the hyperreality of it all.

Putting his lips to her ears as the song continued, he whispered, "Do you know I play the *darabukkah?*"

The totally unexpected comment had her gasping, "Can I have a demonstration later?"

"Only if you promise to dance for me."

She lurched as if he'd scalded her. And he had. He'd injected a whole scene of abandoned sensuality into her imagination. Of her, in an explicitly revealing belly-dancing costume, undulating in a fever to the carnal rhythm, getting hotter with every move before he pulled her on top of him, thrust up into her and rode her into oblivion....

The music stopped, bringing her runaway imaginings to

a grinding halt. Then the *ma'zoon* came forward to begin the marriage ritual. *It was really happening.*

Mohab took her hand in his and the cleric covered their clasped fingers in a pristine white cloth, placing his palm atop them and intoning the marriage declarations. They repeated only the last parts after him, each accepting the other as a spouse. As the cleric stepped away, she thought that was it and she'd managed to survive the ritual without further upheavals. But before she could move, Mohab took her other hand in his.

Looking soulfully into her eyes, his voice rang out to fill the hall, deep and reverent. "That was what any man pledges to any woman he marries. But *my* pledge to you is that you have all of me, have always had all of me and will always have all of me. All that I own, all that I do and all that I am."

She stared up at him, nothing in her bursting heart and chaotic mind translating into words, let alone anything as evocative as what he'd just said. It was all she could do to remain on her feet as the crowd roared with applause again.

In a tumult over what he'd just said, wondering if it had been for show or if it could possibly be true, she watched the Aal Kussaimi tribe elder climb up onto the platform.

He announced that by the unanimous vote of all tribes of Jareer, Mohab was appointed as king of their land, with his heirs after him inheriting the title.

After that, she could barely register anything as the cacophony rose to deafening levels while every tribe elder came up to kiss Mohab's shoulder and offer him the symbol of their tribe, pledging their allegiance and obedience.

Then only she and Mohab remained, and he was talking.

"By the responsibility you granted me, and the privilege you bestowed on me, as your king, I pledge I will rule with justice and mercy, doing everything in my power to fulfill your aspirations and achieve your prosperity." He led her to the edge of the platform. "As my first decree as king of Jareer, I give you my one treasure to rule beside me, in her wisdom and compassion, your queen...Jala Aal Masood."

Cheers rocked the hall, rising to thundering levels as Mohab smashed the region's every ban on displays of public affection and devoured her in a deeply explicit kiss.

Without hesitation, she sank into the rough demand, the ecstasy of his taste and feel. She *would* take it all with him, every second, every breath, every spark of his desire, and make a reservoir of memories for the life ahead devoid of all of that, of him.

Amid a storm of cheering led by her family, he finally relinquished her lips. Then, grinning down at her, eyes blazing with exhilaration, he shouted to her over the din, "Shall we give them the *joloos* they're after?"

Nodding, his enthusiasm infecting her, she rushed after him to their thrones. After he'd seated her in hers, he came down before her on one knee, his eyes roiling with hunger as he kissed her hand. Then he whispered something she couldn't hear. But she read it on his lips. *"Maleekati."*

My queen.

Somehow she didn't burst into tears. But she knew the memory of this moment would fuel weeping jags far into her future, probably till the day she died.

With one last kiss on her hand, he rose to his feet and a hush descended, as if everyone held their breath. She knew just how they felt. Her breath clogged in her lungs as she watched him glide to his throne with the regality of a king born. Then, sweeping his *abaya* aside, he sat down.

Still holding his *abaya* back with a hand at his hip, he leaned forward to prop his right hand over his knee and struck a pose, a display of grandeur and entitlement that would be the standard for every king who came after him.

After he was satisfied everyone had enough photo and video documentation, he turned to her, his smile flaring again. "How about we feed all these enthusiastic people? They've yelled enough for their dinners, don't you think?"

Suddenly she was spluttering with laughter, then with surprise as she found herself plucked from her seat and up into his arms. He descended the steps, with her cradled against him as if she weighed nothing, and waded through the growing din of approval as people parted to let him pass.

The world spun with every thud of his powerful steps, with his feel and scent. Hoping she didn't mess her face or his clothes too much, she clung around his neck, burying her face in his chest, letting him take her wherever he wished.

Excitement swelled as he whisked her outside the citadel walls, where the gigantic wedding tent had been erected in the clearing overlooking Zahara, which was celebrating their new king and his wedding in the most delightful way.

Under a rising full moon, every dwelling in town had its windows open, and in each room blazed a light with a different color, turning the hills they were built over into a spread of glowing gemstones as far as the eye could see.

Then they came to the tent that looked like a fairy castle made of malleable materials, its whiteness silvered by moonbeams and gilded by the flickering flames of the thousand torches surrounding it at a safe distance. It was so big it would accommodate the three thousand people who were attending from the three kingdoms and the world.

The inside was adorned in the same color scheme of her bridal clothes, the rich tones giving everything a deep luxury bordering on decadence. Mohab carried her past hundreds of tables spread with satin tablecloths, lanterns, flowers, the finest local pottery and blown glass, all in vibrant, complementing colors. Then he was setting her down in their *kousha,* a gilded arabesque "marital cage," open on one side so they'd preside over the celebrations.

Right in front of them was the biggest dance floor she'd ever seen covered in hundreds of hand-woven *keleems*.

As soon as everyone took their places around the semi-circular tables, affording everyone the best view of the action, Mohab gestured for dinner to be served, and hundreds of waiters poured from every opening of the tent holding huge serving plates under brass domed covers. Her family and his were in the first row of tables across the dance floor. Her family looked so elated, it twisted the shard in her heart deeper. She brought it under control as she contemplated *his* family. Everyone, including that old goat King Hassan, looked happy with the whole thing. Everyone except Najeeb.

He hadn't talked to her again since the engagement, but his disapproval grated on her every nerve. Najeeb had long come to terms with what his father had done, yet another of his parent's ongoing transgressions that he'd had to put up with all his life. It was *Mohab* he couldn't forgive. Najeeb also couldn't understand why Jala was giving Mohab a second chance after everything that had happened.

As every hurt she'd ever suffered began rushing to her eyes, Mohab tugged at her. The music started to an overpowering rhythm and dozens of young men in flowing beige robes and red headdresses rushed in to form lines. Many women followed to face them, wearing beige-and-garnet dresses and head covers embroidered in cross-stitch designs. Then one of the most energetic folk dances she'd ever seen commenced, one she hadn't witnessed during all the entertainment they'd had in the past two weeks. It must be one reserved for big occasions.

As if reading her mind, Mohab shouted over the music. "That's a special dance for weddings. You haven't seen one before because they postponed all weddings to focus on ours."

As he talked he started clapping, urging her to clap,

too. She did and was soon swept up in the unbridled energy of the performance. Then her family and all of his, except Najeeb, were rushing to the middle of the dance floor, uninhibitedly imitating the steps and soon becoming one with the choreography.

Suddenly the dancers streamed toward her and Mohab, the women converging on her and the men on Mohab.

"You put them up to this!" she accused laughingly, as she was carried on their wave away from him.

He gestured to her, feigning innocence. Then the two waves of dancers rushed toward each other with them in the middle, met then receded, leaving only her and Mohab together, with their families forming a circle around them. Guffawing, he caught her by the waist and swung her round and round, then put her back on the ground and prodded her to dance with him. Recalling long-unpracticed dance steps from Judar, she was soon moving with him to the primal, blood-pounding beat, her heart booming exuberantly in her chest. Finding herself transported into another realm where nothing existed but him, she felt his eyes dominating her, luring her, inflaming her, as he moved *with* her. It felt as if he was connected to her on fundamental levels, as if it was his will that powered her body.

The dances went on and on, interspersed with brief pauses to snatch refreshments and bites of food, then resuming. At one point, the singers handed mikes to each of the celebrity dancers to sing part of the songs. Mohab, of course, sang his motherland's songs perfectly, but when she warbled through her own effort, the kind crowd still roared in approval.

At some point the music came to an end, and she couldn't tell how much time had passed, minutes or hours. It felt as though she was wading in a dream. Then hundreds of people were shaking her hands or kissing her, insisting they'd never enjoyed themselves like this before. Even her family said this rivaled the delight of their own weddings.

Then Mohab disappeared from her side.

Eleven

Before alarm could descend on Jala, her brothers swept her into a 4x4 and drove with her into the desert.

As Farooq drove and Shehab sat beside him, Kamal accompanied her in the back. She nestled into him, still stunned by everything that had happened, endorphins and adrenaline fogging her brain. She didn't even ask where they were taking her. It had to be to Mohab.

Then the car stopped and Kamal pulled her out, and there he was. Mohab. A dozen feet away, at the top of three-foot-wide stone steps leading to a columned patio that wrapped around a one-level adobe lodge. Fiery light glowed behind its closed windows.

His hair rustled around his head like silk, and his *abaya* billowed around his body like the wings of a preternatural bird of prey, with him in the middle of the enchantment, her every fantasy come to life.

Then he spoke, his voice as deep as the desert night enveloping them. "*Skokrunn ya asdeka'ee* for delivering your most valued treasure into my safekeeping. In return for this privilege and trust, I owe you everything."

"Oh, you certainly do," Farooq said, chuckling.

Shehab nodded. "And we have a lifetime to collect."

Kamal rounded it all up. "And don't think we won't."

Mohab bowed his head, his palm spread over his heart in pledge. "I'm counting on it."

With senses fixed on him, she barely registered her brothers kissing her one last time, then driving away.

As their vehicle receded, she forced wobbling legs to move toward Mohab. He wasn't smiling. Or moving. He stood there, his gaze roasting her alive, making her feel he was memorizing her down to her last cell.

"Is this another tradition in Jareer?" she whispered, her voice loud in her ears in the desert's pervasive silence. "Grooms here don't go to the trouble of sweeping their brides away but have their families provide delivery services?"

He smiled then. She didn't know how she remained on her feet with the eruption of arousal.

Ya Ullah...how was it possible to want that much?

He came down a step, then another, his movements tranquil, as if he was afraid she'd bolt if he moved too fast. He reached out a hand to her with the same care.

"Welcome to my sanctuary, *ya ajaml aroos fel kone*."

The way he said *the most beautiful bride in the universe* had her stumbling into his embrace. "One of your lairs?"

"Back to the predator motif?"

"I do feel I'm walking into a starving wolf's den," she confessed.

"That's perfectly true. I *will* gobble you up."

"I'm counting on it."

At her giving him back his words, a chuckle rumbled deep in his chest. "Everything you say or do rouses unprecedented reactions from me." His eyes suddenly sobered. "And after all these years, after I first laid eyes on you and wanted you—but thought I could never have you—here you are, my bride, in my sanctuary where I have never let another."

Shying away from dwelling on his declarations, she focused on his statement about this place. It was that vital and exclusive to him. That had to be why she felt as if her essence was flowing through the ground beneath her feet to forever mingle with this place. Why she felt she'd never belong anywhere else again but in this land, with this man.

She stared up at him, towering above her, swathed in moonlight, as one with the desert and the night, unattainable as the stars. But the universe was giving him to her for now. Sort of on loan. Not having him forever meant she only had to wring every minute with him of all it had of pleasure and intimacy.

Surging against him, she buried her face where his top was open, teeth pulling gently at the muscled power beneath, catching in the perfect cover of silky hair. "Here I am."

"And what you do to me…." Groaning, he swept her up in his arms, made her feel weightless.

She clung to him, burying her lips in any part of him she reached. "Show me, Mohab. Everything I do to you. Everything you need from me. Show me everything, do it all to me."

His growl was savage this time as he took her lips, making her nerves fire in unison.

He relinquished her lips only to stride into the lodge. Kicking the door closed behind them, he swept through a dimly lit corridor that made her feel as if he was taking her deeper into a wizard's den. Which he was. He'd always practiced magic on her. And for the next six months, she'd revel in surrendering to his spell—until the enchantment expired.

She now surrendered to the experience, every foot deeper making her realize for the first time what it meant to *have* a sanctuary. This place. Where he was.

It was as far as could be from the opulence of the palace of Judar or the ancient majesty of his citadel in Jareer. It was composed of elements of the desert, unpolished and unpretentious, and more evocative and atmospheric than those mind-boggling edifices for its starkness and simplicity.

He took her into a great room that seemed to comprise the whole place, apart from a kitchen and bathroom. It had stone walls and adobe floors, and was strewn with thick, hand-woven *keleems*. On one side was a settee with a long table in front of it spread with serving dishes on gentle flames. A fireplace presided over the area, its fires leaping in a hypnotic dance, with the other sources of illumination, brass lamps, on every surface. A mosaic incense burner emitting musk and amber was hanging by thick copper chains from the beamed ceiling.

On the other side of the room was the bed. A ten-by-ten-foot, two-foot-high concrete platform with a thick mattress on top of it was draped in the only luxurious touch around—solid dark gold satin sheets, pillows and covers.

He lowered her down on top of it, then mounted it and brooded down at her as he removed his *abaya* and top, muscles rippling beneath his polished skin, his face all noble planes and harsh slashes and grim hunger, all of him painfully male and beautiful. And hers. For now.

She scrambled to her knees, needing to be rid of her own shackles. She'd removed only the veil when he knelt in front of her, stopping her, his sure, deft hands replacing her clumsy ones. She moaned in protest. "You took *your* clothes off when I spent the whole night promising myself I'd do it."

"You can dress and undress me from now on. But I

spent the whole night having minor coronaries every time I looked at you in this getup, betting myself I'd get it off you in ten seconds flat."

And he did. He got the dress off as if by magic, his eyes on every part he exposed, making her feel purely feminine and utterly desirable. Then he moved around her so he was enveloping her from the back, his hard flesh plastered to her flaming back, his harder erection digging into her buttocks through his pants, making her feel contained… dominated.

His breath steamed down her neck as he whispered, "You want me to show you what I wanted to do to you during those three weeks of torture?"

Her nod was shamelessly frantic. "Yes, yes, show me. Do it all."

"I wanted to catch you, wherever I found you, and do this…." His hand cupped her breast, squeezing until she moaned and arched back, thrusting against his erection, making him growl and snap his teeth over her shoulder. "And this…." The other hand slid down over her abdomen to cup her mound, his fingers delving between her molten feminine lips, finding her entrance, slipping up her flowing readiness.

Her cry rang around the lodge.

His chuckle into her neck was unadulterated sensual devilry. His fingers twisted inside her, making her grind into him, desperate for assuagement. "I take only verbal requests. Graphic ones."

She'd give him graphic. "I want you buried all the way to my womb. I want you to ride me until you shatter me, until I wring your life essence from you."

He snatched his hand from her insides, the withdrawal as exquisite as the plunge. "I changed my mind. Be graphic later. Right now I might have a major coronary."

The sound of his zipper sliding down screeched through

her nerves. Moistness gushed from her eyes and core when his erection thudded against her back, hot and hard and heavy. Mohab. Here. With her. Her husband. For now.

He thrust against her, up and down, burning a furrow in her buttocks and back. "Here I am, everything you need. Take all of it inside you, take me whole, as I take you."

With what felt like the last heartbeat left in her, she turned, rose and sank on him. A cry of welcome rose from her center outward. His erection felt as big as a fist forging inside her. Filled beyond capacity, she writhed against him, pain and pleasure amalgamating into an indecipherable mass. She'd never get used to how he felt inside her, to the sensations his invasion wrung from her every nerve.

Delirious with the feeling of reclamation, she sobbed it all out to him. How he felt inside her, what he did to her, how he inundated her with exquisite pleasure. He only gave her more, thrusting up, harder, faster, forging new depths inside her, panting his own confessions.

The pressure built in her loins with each word, each abrading slide and thrust, spread from that elusive focus of madness he hit over and over. She rode him harder, each thrust layering sensation until she was buried, incoherent, insane for her release from the aching spiral of urgency.

Then it started, like shock waves heralding a detonation too far to be felt yet. Ripples spread from the outside in, pushing everything to her center, compacting it into a pinpoint of desperation. He plunged into her, taking her into one more perfect fusion…and it came. The spike of shearing pleasure, followed by slam after slam of satisfaction.

He pitched her forward, crammed a pillow beneath her stomach, angling her hips upward, then pounded into her wracking convulsions, pouring over her gushing pleasure with the long, hard bursts of his own release.

The next moments or hours, as pleasure raged, they strained against each other, shuddering all over, driving him deeper inside her than he'd ever been, until she felt they'd dissolved into each other.

Then the intensity broke, eased and everything receded, left her replete, complete, spiraling into oblivion....

It was morning when she came to. He had knocked her out for hours this time. And he was again propped beside her, watching her with a smile of supreme gratification.

She stretched luxuriously against him, rubbing her legs against his, delighting in finding him fully aroused. "Sorry I zonked out on you. Not what I planned at all."

"That was the best wedding night gift you could have given me. Lovemaking so explosive it pleasures us both into oblivion. *Aih,* I was knocked out right after you were."

Her lips spread, bliss humming in her bones. "You mean *I* knocked you out."

His indulgence deepened until she drowned in it. "That you surely did. I just woke up. I've never slept that well in...probably ever."

Her hands roamed his face, his head, shoulders, arms and back, reveling in every inch of him. "Anytime. And I want you to take that literally. I want you *any*time, all the time."

"Habibati." His growl went down her throat as he took her lips, pressed her under him and came fully over her.

And he took her up on her offer, plunging into her without preliminaries, knowing she'd be molten with need for him, would love his urgency, his ferocity. She more than loved it, she was mad for it, the fullness and the power and the domination of him. Just a few unbridled thrusts hurled her into ecstasy all over again. And he joined her in the abyss of pleasure, roaring his completion, jetting his seed inside her until he filled her.

He spoke as soon as she opened her eyes. "All these years, all I wanted was to have you again, have what we had, what kept me starving for you. Now I have you again, and it's not the same." Her heart thudded. Did he mean…? "It's way better. When I never thought there could be better."

Her heart filled with so much she couldn't reveal. But she could tell him at least one thing. "It *is* way better."

She didn't go on to say that she believed it would be that way only at first, with six years of frustration behind the initial explosiveness, before everything leveled then tapered off.

Needing to take them away from such disturbing discussions, she asked one thing that had been worrying her since she'd arrived here. "Why didn't you bring the kitties?"

His laugh revved beneath her ear. "Not even I would bring cats to my wedding night." He laughed again. "Though I might have considered it if the place had another room. They're good about staying in another room if I want to be alone…or with you, like that first night back in Judar. But they're in their favorite new place back in the citadel with all those places to explore."

Another worry struck her. "What if someone leaves a door to their quarters open? Or a window? Or if one zooms out when someone goes in to feed them or…"

Mohab swept her in a soothing caress from shoulder to buttock. "I've left as many paranoid instructions about keeping them safe as your heart can desire."

Still not satisfied, she said, "Can we check on them?"

"We certainly can. Mizar would even come to the phone. *Then* I will devour you again, and this time longer and harder, just for being so protective of my kitties."

She gasped as he turned her onto her back and reached over her for his pants on the ground. "Aren't they mine, too, now?"

"Oh, yes, they are. They are part of me, and I've already given you carte blanche to me and mine."

And as he called his people to fulfill her wish, she threaded her aching fingers through his silky hair, and wondered.

Did he mean everything he said to her the way it sounded? Did he really feel this way about her? The way she felt about him? Did she even want him to feel that way?

No. She didn't. She wanted to have this with him, let them enjoy each other as much as they wanted, as much as they could and nothing else. For six long—and way too short—months.

Twelve

"Can you believe six months have passed so fast?"

Jala felt the smile beginning to sink its claws into her flesh as she handed Sette to Ala'a, Kamal and Aliyah's five-year-old son. It gave her something to do so she wouldn't answer Aliyah's exclamation.

For what could she say? That there was nothing else she'd thought about every minute of these six months. That the days were passing so *horribly* fast? And now that the six months were up, she felt as if her very life was, too?

Aliyah threw herself beside Jala on the couch, grinning at her son's retreating back as he rushed to his sister in the other room with the last piece in his treasure, the tolerant Sette, having now collected all four cats.

"I thought once I got the kids four cats, too, they'd stop demanding to visit you to see yours every week, but no… your foursome are their first loves."

"One more thing to thank the cats for, then, making

me see you all much more frequently than I would have without them."

Aliyah laughed. "We all thought we loved cats, but you and Mohab put us to shame. Last time I saw Mohab he said you'll adopt dozens more as soon as you settle your schedules and make the citadel your base, because cats hate traveling."

Every word fell on her like a blow so that she almost gasped in relief when Aliyah's phone rang.

Thankful for the respite, she contemplated her sister-in-law. Aliyah was her very antithesis, glowing with health and happiness, her world built on the unshakable foundation of Kamal's love and of her certain future with him. While she... She'd been counting down the days she had left with Mohab and was withering inside. She'd taken to putting on makeup to prevent outward signs from showing.

Watching Aliyah melt with love as she talked to Kamal, she couldn't be happier for them, but at the same time, it made her own despondence deepen until it suffocated her.

With a last intimate whisper, Aliyah ended the call. "Kamal sends hugs and kisses. But insisted I tell you that your husband conned him."

Alarm burst inside her chest.

Aliyah went on. "He says Mohab said he doesn't know the first thing about dealing with the executive realities of running a kingdom, especially one that is growing and changing as much and as fast as Jareer. He now believes Mohab's protestations were just total pretense so he'd get him involved—not because he needs his help, but to get on his good side, so he'd help him have you, and now continues to rely on his input for your sake, too."

"I don't believe this is true...."

Aliyah waved her hand, her smile widening. "Kamal said you'd think that, but he knows a man who'd do anything for his woman when he sees one. And take it from me, that 'twin' of yours has…extensive experience and insight in that arena."

Any other woman would have considered this everything worth living for. Knowing the man she loved with all her being felt the same. But having someone corroborate the depth of Mohab's involvement, which she'd been becoming more certain of with each passing minute, only sank her deeper into despair.

"Kamal would have respected the hell out of Mohab for achieving what no one believed could be done around here, let alone in this time frame. But the fact that he has you at the top of his priorities makes Kamal feel progressively more smug that he pegged Mohab right from the first meeting, when he came proposing peace between our kingdoms…and offering it all as your *mahr*."

Time did keep proving that she and Kamal were identical. For it had substantiated that she'd pegged Mohab right, too, from that first second she'd laid eyes on him. That he was everything she would ever want in a man, everything she could—and did—love, respect and admire. And that everything that happened to make her believe otherwise had been just tragic mistakes and misunderstandings.

Contrary to what she'd tried to convince herself of in the years of alienation, that Mohab was unfeeling by necessity, he actually turned off his feelings on demand only in his work. In his personal life, with her, she'd never known anyone who was more in touch with his emotions and so generous with demonstrating them. And it had been killing her to realize how she'd misjudged him, what she'd done to him. What she'd have to do still.

Time had also proved she was a superlative actress. Not even Mohab, Kamal and now Aliyah, the people who loved her most, suspected there was a thing wrong with her.

Demonstrating her obliviousness, Aliyah went on, "I think you're making one hell of a queen, too. It's like you're made to rule this specific place beside your man, your every skill and quality just what it needs. I'm so impressed by the originality of your social and educational projects and the effects they're already having. I need you to teach me how to translate that to Judar."

And she could take no more. "Please, Aliyah, stop."

The pain in her voice had her sister-in-law sitting up in alarm. "What's wrong, Jala?"

Everything, she wanted to scream.

Up until Aliyah's visit today, she'd been escaping making a decision, thinking she could go on for a while more, maybe another month, maybe another six.

But after what Aliyah had told her earlier, so offhandedly, believing it would be nothing to concern her, she'd been feeling her world had already ended.

She swallowed past the burning coal that used to be her larynx. "I want to tell you something, Aliyah. And I need you to make Kamal understand that it is in no way Mohab's fault...."

"How are my darlings today?"

Mohab walked into their bedroom, taking off the band that held his hair in that severe ponytail, his smile flooding the soothingly lit chamber.

By the time he reached the bed where Jala was sitting with the four cats arranged all around her, he'd stripped off his jacket and shirt. Then he threw himself down beside her, grinning, spreading himself for his cats to climb all over him, stroking and kissing them. After a purring storm interlude, he turned his focus to her.

Before she succumbed and attacked him in her desperation for his feel and passion, he preempted her, dragged her down to him, surging up to take her lips as she tumbled across him.

Knowing, now that the kissing had started, neither

Mohab nor Jala would want them around, the cats jumped off the bed and prowled out to the quarters' farthest sitting room.

"Habibati, wahashteeni..." Mohab groaned into her lips as he swept her around and bore down on her.

I missed you, too, my love almost burst onto her lips. But as she'd done for the past six months, she swallowed back the endearments and the confessions until they'd scarred her forever with the intensity of their need for release, with the necessity of withholding them.

Mohab had them both naked in seconds, and she groped for him, opened herself for his possession as he cupped her buttocks and thrust inside her. This fever was a continuation of last night's conflagration, no need for buildup, just an instantaneous and ferocious plunge into delirium. He was soon pounding inside her, his force and momentum building along with her cries of abandon until it all exploded into a blaze of intensity. She remained conscious this time as he collapsed on top of her, his weight completing the magic and delivering the final injury.

When she couldn't take it anymore, she fidgeted beneath him. He rose off her, separating their bodies. For the last time. As she had to make it.

She took the plunge. "The six months are up tomorrow."

A slow smile spread on his heartbreakingly beautiful face. "So they are. How about extending for another six months?" He plucked her lips. "Then another?" Another pull, harder, deeper. "And so on and on?" His teeth sank into her trembling flesh, sending shards of pleasure and heartache splintering through her. Then he pulled back, grinning. "These constant extensions might be a great idea to renew the novelty and keep the fire raging...*if* we needed help in those departments. Which we don't. None what...so...ever."

"That won't be necessary."

"So you're going for the permanent version straight away. I approve."

"I am actually reinforcing the terms of our marriage. I agreed to six months, then it's over. As it is."

He stilled, the smile faltering on his lips, draining from his eyes. "What do you mean?"

And she smashed her own heart. "I mean I want a divorce."

The sense of suffocating déjà vu closed in on Mohab.

This couldn't be happening again. Not this time. This time he was certain of what she felt for him. Of what they had.

Numb, he sat up. "Joke about anything but that, Jala." When she made no response as she, too, sat up, he tried to find a sign of mischief in her eyes. There was none. "You can't be serious!"

"I am. *Ermi alai yameen al talaag.*"

The oath of divorce. She was asking him to "throw" it at her, ending their marriage.

Ya Ullah...she wasn't joking.

A bewildered groan escaped him. "Why? Why are you doing this? Again?"

"I'm only doing what we agreed on."

"But you can't want the same thing you did six months ago. Just last night, just *now*.... *Ya Ullah*...you've never been more incendiary in my arms."

"You know I could never resist my desire for you. But I have to now. It has to end."

"It wasn't only desire. You *love* me."

"I never said I did."

He opened his mouth to roar a contradiction, then it hit him. Skewered him right through the heart. She'd *never* said it. He'd only assumed she did. From her actions and desire.

He couldn't accept it. Wouldn't. "Even if you don't feel for me what I feel for you, if you want me that much, why leave me?" She only averted her eyes, and the expanding shock shredded his insides. "And if you'd already decided to leave me all along, what was last night and just now all about? Were you giving me one last ride before you walked away?"

She rose from the bed, so slowly, as if she was afraid she'd come apart if she moved any faster. "Let's not make this any worse than it has to be, Mohab."

Again. Just as she'd said almost seven years ago when she was leaving him the first time.

Paralyzed, he watched her reach for the dress he'd yanked off her half an hour ago. When she'd been his. She put it on now, no longer his, had said she'd never really been.

Then she was walking away.

At the door she turned. "I'll go to Judar until you conclude the procedures. Please, don't make any further personal contact. Goodbye, Mohab."

"Did you put her up to this?

Najeeb rose as Mohab burst into his office, placed both palms flat on his desk, his pose confrontational. "I assume you're talking about Jala."

"It won't take much to snap the last tethers of my sanity, Najeeb. Then I won't be responsible for what I do."

"King of Jareer or not, you're on my turf. Even if you weren't, you don't threaten me and walk away in one piece."

"I'm not threatening you, I'm promising you. If you're the reason why Jala left me…"

Najeeb straightened, a vicious smile of satisfaction spreading on his face. "So she finally did. Good for her. She should have never been with you in the first place."

"I swear, Najeeb…" Mohab's apoplectic surge drained. "You mean you had no idea she did, or *would?*"

"Do you have such a low opinion of the woman you married, you think someone can put her up to anything, let alone something like this?"

"*No.* But…" Anger deserted him, leaving him enervated with desperation and confusion, and he sank onto the nearest armchair and dropped his head in his hands, darkness closing in on him. "I don't know. I can't think anymore. I can't find a reason why she left me and I was groping for anything, even if it was insane or impossible. I just want to understand, so I can do something about it." He raised his eyes to Najeeb, who came to stand over him, his gaze pitiless. "I have to stop her, Najeeb. I can't live without her."

"*Ya Ullah,* if I didn't know better, I would have believed you without question, would have run out right now and tried everything I could to bring her back to you. But I *know,* Mohab. So stop your act right now. Now that Jala will no longer be your wife, it releases me from my promise to her."

"What promise?"

"Not to be your enemy. But now I will be, Mohab. I knew you were manipulating her when you announced your engagement out of the blue, but I couldn't object since I realized she was making a decision knowing full well that you were. Then it seemed as if your marriage was real, and happy, and I no longer knew what to think." He narrowed his eyes to dangerous slits. "But if she left you, then you must have dealt her another unspeakable injury. And for that alone, Mohab, no matter what it takes, I will destroy you."

"*B'Ellahi*…what are you talking about?"

"About how you set her up in the past. She made me promise never to confront you, wanted the ugly page turned and forgotten. I honored her request till this moment."

Mohab shook his head. "I know you found out and told her, and that was one of the reasons she left me then. She told me everything the very first night I saw her again. It's why I thought it might have been something you said to her that made her end it this time, too." He exhaled roughly. "This…and the dread that never went away—that I did come between you in the past, that your feelings for each other went beyond friendship.…"

Najeeb wrenched his shoulder, his face contemptuous. "You think Jala could have had emotions for me and still came to your bed? Betraying us both?"

"I said it was a dread, not a suspicion. She's the most upstanding person I know, the most forthright."

"She is. I share a bond with her that was forged in the fire of our lives' worst experience and later nurtured by our kindred natures. There was never the least romantic involvement on either of our sides, as I told my foolish father. You should have both believed in *my* forthrightness and that if my emotions for her had been of that nature, I would never have denied them."

"That's why I'm going insane. Because I believe in *her*. And everything she did, said…indicated she'd forgiven me, proved she loved me now, even if she never truly did in the past."

"She did love you in the past. So completely your deception destroyed her."

He shook his head. "She told me what she felt for me wasn't strong enough to counterbalance her aversion to commitment and her fear that I was a threat to her independence. Her discovery of my deception was just the last straw."

"Then she told you a lie, so you wouldn't know the

depth of her past involvement and what your betrayal cost her."

Mohab gaped at Najeeb, a vice squeezing around his heart. If this was true, then he *had* hurt her more than he'd ever realized. Which made her being with him again at all a miracle. Was that her revenge? To make him fall as fully in love with her as she'd fallen for him once, then give him a taste of his own poison?

But…no. She *wouldn't* do that.

Najeeb went on, ending his confusion…and delivering a crippling blow. "When I told her the truth, she pretended that you hadn't succeeded in seducing her, that I saved her in time to salvage her dignity. But then I discovered the depth of your exploitation of her when I stumbled on her in a relief mission in Colombia…and found her pregnant."

By the time he arrived in Judar, Mohab felt he'd lost whatever remained of his sanity. On receiving him, Kamal had said he didn't care how this had happened, only that Mohab resolve it or have him as an enemy for life.

Mohab had told him to stand in line.

Now he entered Jala's quarters and found her standing at the French windows. She spoke as soon as he closed the door.

"I told you not to do this, Mohab, not to force another confrontation on me. I have nothing more to say to you."

And all his shock and anguish bled out of him. "I almost went insane all those months I couldn't find you after you left me. Now I know I couldn't because you did everything to disappear. So I wouldn't find out you were pregnant."

"You went to Najeeb." A ragged breath left her. "But you're wrong. I disappeared so I wouldn't cause my family a scandal. I didn't think you would bother with me again."

Every word made him realize he had dealt her an indelible injury.

But right now, there was one injury in particular that he needed to heal. "I want you to tell me what happened to our baby."

"What do you think happened? That I gave him away?"

Him. It had been a boy. The knife hacking his vitals twisted. "I think you lost him. I want you to tell me how."

"It was a landslide while driving up a mountain in Colombia. The jeep rolled over into the valley. One passenger died...and I lost the baby. I was seven months pregnant."

Her telegraphic account, condensing her horrific experience, felt like bullets. "And you hated me that much, you didn't think to tell me you were carrying my baby? Distrusted me so totally, you didn't even think it a possibility I'd want to be there for you after your ordeal?"

Another ragged exhalation. "I believed I didn't matter to you either way, so I assumed you wouldn't have cared if I carried your baby. And that you would have probably been relieved I lost it."

He squeezed his eyes. He'd hurt her even worse than his worst projections. "Is this why you're leaving me? Because you still don't believe I care?"

"I left because we had a deal."

And he stormed toward her, his every nerve firing as he grasped her shoulders, felt her again. "To hell with that deal. I never really meant it when I first proposed it, and I faced the truth of what I always wanted right before our engagement. *Ahwaaki, ya hayati, aashagek wa abghaki bekolli jawarehi.* I love you, and I worship and crave you with every spark of my being. You're not in my heart, you *are* my heart. And I can't live without my heart."

She wrenched herself free from his grasp, her features suddenly contorting out of control, her voice strangled with tears. "That's what you say now, what you think you mean. But you're not only a man, not only a prince, you're a king now. You will need an heir. An heir I *can't* give you."

He gaped at her, a cascade of mutilating suspicions crashing in his mind. Her next words ended them, solidifying them into terrible reality.

"My miscarriage was so traumatic, at such an advanced stage, the doctors told me I'd never have children again."

This was it. The dark secret that explained it all. All the pain he'd felt from her and could never account for.

When he'd learned she'd been pregnant, he'd thought losing their baby explained it. But it wasn't only the loss, the injury, but the permanent scar. She'd lost their baby, and any hope of having another.

He stared at her as her tears began to flow, as her shoulders began to shake, at a total loss.

What could he do to mitigate her anguish?

He heard his voice, choking on his own agony. "I don't *want* an heir, *ya hayati.* I didn't inherit my title, I was chosen for it based on merit, and when the time comes for me to step down, I will pass the throne to whomever deserves it."

A shaking hand wiped at her tears. "You do need an heir. Aliyah told me King Hassan is withholding signing any treaties until he knows the reason he blessed our marriage, the blood-mixing heir, is a reality. She wasn't worried, but only because she thinks we're postponing having children voluntarily."

And then he exploded. "To hell with my uncle and Saraya and the peace treaty. To hell with Judar and Jareer and everyone in them. I only care about you."

"You can't say that. Now that you're king, you owe it to your subjects to keep the peace in their kingdom. I'll be what stands in the way of your achieving it."

"I *will* keep the peace, and it won't be by bowing to any backward tribal demands. I only pretended to so it would give me a chance to approach you again."

She shook her head as she escaped his grasp, tears falling faster. "Even if you do, you *will* want a family...."

"We *already* have a family—me and you and our furry babies, and we'll have as many more as you want. And if you long for the human kind of kid, we'll try. The doctors' verdict doesn't have to be final...."

"It is. I didn't use protection, hoping they were wrong. They weren't. There is no hope."

"Maybe there will be with minimum intervention. If there isn't, or you don't want even that, I don't care."

"I can't, Mohab...I can't let you give up your right to have a child. I can't let you give *anything* up."

"But *I* want to give up *everything* for you, *ya habibat hayati*." She shook so hard, her tears splashed over his hands, burning him through to his marrow. He clamped her shaking head in trembling hands, tilted her face up toward his. He had to convince her, stop her from leaving him, destroying them both. "You carried my baby inside you, nourished and nurtured him in your body and with your essence. You wanted him and loved him, even when you thought I never wanted or loved you. And I wasn't there for you...."

A hiccup tore out of her. "I was the one who pushed you away, who made it impossible for you to find me. You looked for me, even thinking I never really loved you...."

"I should have looked more efficiently, not let my anxiety mess up my methods. You can't imagine how much it hacks at me to know you were pregnant, without me, and then had to go through the pain and desolation and loss... *Ya Ullah, ya rohi*...if I can't give you all my life in recompense, I would end it in penance."

"Don't say this.... *Ya Ullah*...don't...feel this way."

"I do feel this way. And as far as I am concerned, you *have* given me a son, and *we* lost him. And now I grieve with you as I should have at the time, and we cling to each other even more, and forever."

"No." Her shriek of agony pierced him as she stumbled around and staggered away.

He hurtled after her, caught her back and crushed her to him, out of his mind now with dread, begging her over and over. *"La tseebeeni tani, la tseebeeni tani abaddan."*

Don't leave me again, don't leave me ever again.

Mohab's litany sheared through her, and his tears—his *tears*—rained over her face, mingling with hers, singeing her soul. She never thought she'd ever see them. And now that she did, felt their agony rain down her flesh, she couldn't bear them, would do anything to never see them again.

But she had to do this for him. He would come to regret his emotional outburst when his head cleared and his passion cooled. He'd sooner or later long for a child of his flesh and blood. And she'd be what deprived him of fulfilling this need. He'd come to resent her for it. It was better for her to die, to leave him now than to live with him till this came to pass.

She pushed out of his arms, shaking apart, tears a stream draining her life force. "I never suspected you loved me as much as I love you, Mohab. That was why I agreed to marry you. I wanted to have some more time with you, give you the closure you said you needed, then disappear from your life again. If I suspected you felt the same, I wouldn't have done this to you." A sob tore out of her depths. "Please, believe me, I never thought I'd hurt you. But once I realized you had become emotionally involved, I knew it was better to hurt you temporarily than hurt you for the rest of your life. When I'm gone, in time, you will forget me."

He groaned as if she'd just stabbed him. "If I never

forgot you when I thought you didn't love me, when you weren't my wife, you think I'd ever forget you now?"

"You *have* to."

"Would *you* have left me? If you discovered I couldn't give you a child? Especially if you knew I couldn't on account of an injury you caused me?"

"You had nothing to do with my accident. I won't have you feeling guilty over this."

"I *am* guilty. Of injuring your belief in me and in your own self-worth. Anything that happened from that moment forward is my responsibility, my guilt."

She wiped furiously at her streaming eyes. "I once held you responsible, too, but I was wrong. If there was guilt, then I share it in full. I didn't give you a chance to defend yourself, intended to deprive you of your child. I deserve what happened to me...."

"*B'Ellahi*...you were a victim in all this, *my* victim."

At his desperate shout, her sobs ratcheted until they drove her down to the ground.

Jala gazed up at him as he stood over her, looking as if his heart had spilled on the ground, and she wailed, "If you love me, Mohab, let me set you free. I'm not leaving you. This time I'm begging you to let me go."

He let Jala go.

But only to set the plan to get her back in motion. Now that he knew she loved him, too, he was never letting her go.

He had called a summit of all the people who were players in this mess. His uncle, Najeeb and her family. They were all convened in Kamal's stateroom. Jala was there, too. This had been the last favor Kamal had said he'd ever do for him.

He walked in, swept them all in a careless gaze, before he focused on Jala. She looked pinched and drained, her beloved eyes extinguished. It nearly drove him to his knees, how much she suffered, how injured and scarred she was. He wanted to lay down his life so she'd be whole again, so she'd stop feeling any deficiency. But since he couldn't undo the damage, he could only move heaven and earth, dedicate his very life to making it up to her.

He started talking at once. He told them the truth about the past, what he'd done, what he'd cost Jala.

Feeling her brothers' rage boiling over, he went on, "I want you to know that I will accept, even encourage, any punishment you exact from me. But that isn't why I called you here. I did so to inform you that no matter what you do, no matter what happens, I'll part from Jala only when I die."

His uncle heaved up to his feet. "But you have to. I only agreed to the treaty, *and* the marriage…"

"Shut *up*, uncle." His roar made King Hassan sag back to his chair. "*You* didn't agree to anything, I was just humoring you, trying to save your face and avoid your folly. But if you make any more trouble, or if you don't sign the treaty, I will be the one to declare war on you."

"You don't even have an army," his uncle spluttered.

"I'll make one. Or I'll borrow one if it's faster. Jareer is far more important to so many powers today than Saraya, and they would do anything for me if I ask. I bet they'd help me depose you just to be rid of your nuisance. So *enough,* uncle. You've already cost us what your very life doesn't begin to make up for. Take my clemency and never let us hear from you again except as a voice corroborating peace."

His uncle looked shocked to his core. Najeeb, while looking at his father pityingly, seemed to wholly approve.

And he couldn't care less about either of them right now.

He turned to Jala's family. "My happiness, honor and all my hopes lie in whatever will make Jala happy, will honor her and fulfill her hopes. If she wants to try to have children, this is what we'll do. If she wants to adopt…"

"You can't adopt!" That was his uncle again. "It's prohibited by law in our region!"

"Uncle, you are now tampering with the gauge of your life. I won't warn you again. We will adopt as many children as she wishes, if she wishes it. I will give up my throne and two nationalities, and acquire one that will allow me to fulfill her every need." He walked up to Jala, knelt before her. Her whole frame was shaking, her tears like acid in his veins.

"Jala, you *are* my life. I want nothing but you, need nothing but your love. I would only have wanted a child as one more bond with you. I lost our baby, too, but my pain is over your loss. And the only loss that would finish me is if I lose you. Nothing is of any importance to me— not my throne, not my homelands, not my very life—if I don't have you."

Kamal suddenly heaved up to his feet. "This is not for our eyes or ears. Everybody, *out*."

Kamal's barked order had everyone rushing out, everyone except his bewildered uncle giving Mohab bolstering, approving glances. Kamal was the only one who stopped as he passed him, bent to squeeze his shoulder.

Then, dropping a kiss on Jala's shuddering cheek, he whispered to her, "I know when a man would die without his woman, *ya sugheerati.* You got yourself a prime specimen of that rare species. As only you deserve. So just take him back and keep him for life, if you don't want to kill him." He straightened, winked. "If you *do* want to kill him, then by all means, walk away."

Everything that had happened in the past years, everything Jala had suffered, everything she'd shared with Mohab in the past months, everything he'd just said and offered, built inside her until she felt herself overloading. Then Kamal winked teasingly at her, and everything snapped inside her.

And she howled. With laughter.

Mohab's jaw dropped. Kamal only bowed, as if he was taking applause for a job perfectly done, then with another wink, he walked out, too.

Recovering from the shock of her sudden transformation into a hyena, Mohab's smile broke out as he surged up, enveloping her in his arms.

"Ah, *ya habibati*...how I missed your laughter, feared I'd never hear it again."

A snort interrupted her howls. "You're that desperate for me...you call *this*...laughter?"

This drew a chuckle from him before her raucous glee escalated it into laughter, then guffawing.

It was only when she sagged in his arms, still gurgling and sobbing at once, that he stopped, too, storming kisses all over her face, murmuring extravagant endearments and professions of worship before stilling her gasping lips beneath his.

Breathing life and certainty into her once more, he managed to quiet her down. Then, holding her face in his palms, he withdrew, his heart in his still-beseeching eyes.

"I am that desperate and more. I'm also desperate in case you will keep thinking you'd be doing me a favor by walking away, that I can forget you 'in time.' When I wanted you for over ten years, had you only for just over ten months out of those, and couldn't forget you in between, that I never even thought of having anyone but you."

Everything stilled, inside and out. "You mean...?"

"I mean just as you never had anyone else but me, I never had anyone else but you. I'm yours, whether you take me…or leave me. So will you have mercy on both of us and take me, and this time never leave me?"

This was just too…enormous. He'd always been hers, just the way she'd always been his.

Everything inside her crumbling, she threw herself at him, hugged him with all her might, until her arms and heart ached. "I—I never wanted to leave you. I just want you to have everything you need and deserve."

He kissed one eye, then the other. "That's you, and you."

"Ah, *ya habibi*…I've loved you for so long."

He suddenly bombarded her with kisses. "And she says it at last."

Spluttering with laughter again, she gasped, "I made you wade in 'I love yous' in the past."

"Then forced a years-long drought on me in compensation."

"When I thought I would have to leave you, I didn't want to compound the mess with revealing my emotions. And then 'I love you' was no longer adequate to describe what I felt for you since I became your wife. *Ahwak wa abghak wa aashagak, ya roh galbi.*"

His eyes filled again as he heard her confess more than love and adoration and worship, *everything* anyone could feel with the whole of their hearts and minds and souls.

She surged to kiss his eyes, tasting his precious tears, which she swore she'd never cause again.

Withdrawing, she voiced her last lingering fear. "I'm just so scared…."

He wouldn't let her continue, enveloping her again. "That I don't know what I'm talking about? That I'd change my mind? If ten years don't prove to you that I was made to love you, that you are the one thing I need to be happy, I demand another test to prove that to you. The next fifty years."

And she surrendered. To his overwhelming love, to the unimaginable happiness of an inseparable life together... come what may. "If I have those, they're all yours. As I am. Always have been. Always will be."

* * * * *

And if you loved Mohab and Jala's story, check out all the novels in the
MARRIED BY ROYAL DECREE
series from
USA TODAY *bestselling author Olivia Gates*

TEMPORARILY HIS PRINCESS
CONVENIENTLY HIS PRINCESS

All available now from Harlequin Desire!

Don't miss USA TODAY *bestselling author Olivia Gates's*
THE SARANTOS BABY BARGAIN
a BILLIONAIRES AND BABIES *novel, available May 2014*

Available April 1, 2014

#2293 ONE GOOD COWBOY
Diamonds in the Rough • by Catherine Mann
To inherit the family business, CEO Stone McNair must prove he isn't heartless underneath his ruthlessly suave exterior. His trial? Finding homes for rescue dogs. His judge? The ex-fiancée who's heart he broke.

#2294 THE BLACK SHEEP'S INHERITANCE
Dynasties: The Lassiters • by Maureen Child
Suspicious of his late father's nurse when she inherits millions in his father's will, Sage Lassiter is determined to get the truth. Even if he has to seduce it out of her.

#2295 HIS LOVER'S LITTLE SECRET
Billionaires and Babies • by Andrea Laurence
Artist Sabine Hayes fell hard for shipping magnate Gavin Brooks, and when it was over, she found herself pregnant. Now he's come to demand his son—and the passion they've both denied.

#2296 A NOT-SO-INNOCENT SEDUCTION
The Kavanaghs of Silver Glen • by Janice Maynard
The sexy but stoic Liam has headed the Kavanagh family since his reckless father's disappearance two decades ago. But meeting the innocent, carefree Zoe awakens his passions, derailing his sense of duty.

#2297 WANTING WHAT SHE CAN'T HAVE
The Master Vintners • by Yvonne Lindsay
Her best friend's last wish was that Alexis care for her baby—and her husband. So Alexis becomes the nanny, determined to heal this family without falling for the one man she can't have.

#2298 ONCE PREGNANT, TWICE SHY
by Red Garnier
Wealthy Texan Garret Gage promised to protect family friend Kate just as fiercely as her father would have. And he'd been doing just fine, until one night of passion changes everything.

YOU CAN FIND MORE INFORMATION ON UPCOMING HARLEQUIN® TITLES, FREE EXCERPTS AND MORE AT WWW.HARLEQUIN.COM.

HDCNM0314

REQUEST YOUR FREE BOOKS!
2 FREE NOVELS PLUS 2 FREE GIFTS!

HARLEQUIN®

Desire

ALWAYS POWERFUL, PASSIONATE AND PROVOCATIVE

YES! Please send me 2 FREE Harlequin Desire® novels and my 2 FREE gifts (gifts are worth about $10). After receiving them, if I don't wish to receive any more books, I can return the shipping statement marked "cancel." If I don't cancel, I will receive 6 brand-new novels every month and be billed just $4.55 per book in the U.S. or $4.99 per book in Canada. That's a savings of at least 13% off the cover price! It's quite a bargain! Shipping and handling is just 50¢ per book in the U.S. and 75¢ per book in Canada.* I understand that accepting the 2 free books and gifts places me under no obligation to buy anything. I can always return a shipment and cancel at any time. Even if I never buy another book, the two free books and gifts are mine to keep forever.

225/326 HDN F4ZC

Name _____
(PLEASE PRINT)

Address _____ Apt. # _____

City _____ State/Prov. _____ Zip/Postal Code _____

Signature (if under 18, a parent or guardian must sign)

Mail to the **Harlequin® Reader Service:**

IN U.S.A.: P.O. Box 1867, Buffalo, NY 14240-1867
IN CANADA: P.O. Box 609, Fort Erie, Ontario L2A 5X3

**Want to try two free books from another line?
Call 1-800-873-8635 or visit www.ReaderService.com.**

* Terms and prices subject to change without notice. Prices do not include applicable taxes. Sales tax applicable in N.Y. Canadian residents will be charged applicable taxes. Offer not valid in Quebec. This offer is limited to one order per household. Not valid for current subscribers to Harlequin Desire books. All orders subject to credit approval. Credit or debit balances in a customer's account(s) may be offset by any other outstanding balance owed by or to the customer. Please allow 4 to 6 weeks for delivery. Offer available while quantities last.

Your Privacy—The Harlequin® Reader Service is committed to protecting your privacy. Our Privacy Policy is available online at www.ReaderService.com or upon request from the Harlequin Reader Service.

We make a portion of our mailing list available to reputable third parties that offer products we believe may interest you. If you prefer that we not exchange your name with third parties, or if you wish to clarify or modify your communication preferences, please visit us at www.ReaderService.com/consumerschoice or write to us at Harlequin Reader Service Preference Service, P.O. Box 9062, Buffalo, NY 14269. Include your complete name and address.

SPECIAL EXCERPT FROM

Read on for a sneak peek at
USA TODAY *bestselling author*
Maureen Child's
THE BLACK SHEEP'S INHERITANCE,
the debut novel in Harlequin® Desire's
DYNASTIES: THE LASSITERS *series.*

A Wyoming business legend dies and leaves his nurse a
fortune. Now his son wants answers…

"Colleen!"

That deep voice was unmistakable. Colleen had been close to Sage Lassiter only one time before today. The night of his sister's rehearsal dinner. From across that crowded restaurant, she'd felt him watching her. The heat of his gaze had swamped her, sending ribbons of expectation unfurling throughout her body. He'd smiled and her stomach had churned with swarms of butterflies. He'd headed toward her, and she'd told herself to be calm. Cool. But it hadn't worked. Nerves had fired, knees weakened.

And just as he had been close enough to her that she could see the gleam in his eyes, J.D. had had his heart attack and everything had changed forever.

Sage Lassiter *stalked* across the parking lot toward her. He was like a man on a mission. He wore dark jeans, boots and an expensively cut black sport jacket over a long-sleeved white shirt. His brown hair flew across his forehead and his blue eyes were narrowed against the wind. In a few short seconds, he was there. Right in front of her.

She had to tip her head back to meet his gaze and when she did, nerves skated down along her spine.

"I'm so sorry about your father."

A slight frown crossed his face. "Thanks. Look, I wanted to talk to you—"

"You did?" There went her silly heart again, jumping into a gallop.

"Yes. I've got a couple questions…."

Fascination dissolved into truth. Here she was, daydreaming about a gorgeous man suddenly paying attention to her when the reality was he'd just lost his father. As J.D.'s private nurse, she'd be the first he'd turn to.

"Of course you do." Instinctively, she reached out, laid her hand on his and felt a swift jolt of electricity jump from his body to hers.

His eyes narrowed further and she knew he'd felt it, too.

Shaking his head, he said, "No. I don't have any questions about J.D. You went from nurse to millionaire in a few short months. Actually, *you're* the mystery here."

Read more of
THE BLACK SHEEP'S INHERITANCE,
available April 2014
wherever Harlequin® Desire and ebooks are sold.

Copyright © 2014 by Maureen Child